FOR MERCY

(A Morgan Cross FBI Suspense Thriller—Book Sixteen)

BLAKE PIERCE

Blake Pierce

USA Today and #1 bestselling author Blake Pierce is the author of numerous series in the mystery and thriller genres, spanning 10 years of work, including the Jessie Hunt, Ella Dark, Rylie Page, Faith Bold and Rachel Gift series. Blake's most recent latest releases are the Jenna Graves, Alison Payne, Isla Rivers and Kari Blackhorse series.

Please visit blakepierceauthor.com to learn more, join the email list, receive free books, and stay in touch.

SERIES BY BLAKE PIERCE

KARI BLACKHORSE
ISLA RIVERS
ALISON PAYNE
JENNA GRAVES
THE GOVERNESS
RACHEL BLACKWOOD
SHEILA STONE
FINN WRIGHT
MORGAN CROSS
JULIETTE HART
FAITH BOLD
FIONA RED
DAISY FORTUNE
AMBER YOUNG
CAMI LARK
NICKY LYONS
CORA SHIELDS
MAY MOORE
PAIGE KING
VALERIE LAW
RACHEL GIFT
AVA GOLD
A YEAR IN EUROPE
ELLA DARK
LAURA FROST
EUROPEAN VOYAGE
ADELE SHARP
THE AU PAIR
ZOE PRIME
JESSIE HUNT
CHLOE FINE
KATE WISE
THE MAKING OF RILEY PAIGE
RILEY PAIGE
MACKENZIE WHITE
AVERY BLACK
KERI LOCKE

PROLOGUE

The blackness receded like a sluggish tide, revealing slivers of consciousness that pierced Judge Richard Hawthorne's mind. Each pulse of awareness brought with it a fresh wave of agony that radiated from the base of his skull. He tried to swallow, his throat constricting around the metallic tang of blood that coated his tongue.

Hawthorne's nostrils flared, desperately seeking fresh air, but found only staleness tinged with a sharp, chemical odor that made his eyes water. Dust tickled the back of his throat, threatening to trigger a coughing fit. He fought against the urge, instinctively knowing that any sudden movement would only intensify the throbbing in his head.

Where am I? The thought floated through the haze of pain, elusive as smoke. The last thing he remembered was leaving the courthouse, briefcase in hand, heading for his car in the underground parking garage. Then... nothing. A void where his memories should be.

Hawthorne attempted to lift his hand to his aching head, but found his arm wouldn't respond. Panic fluttered in his chest as he strained against an unyielding resistance. Something rough bit into the flesh of his wrists. Leather straps?

No. No, this can't be happening.

His heart rate spiked, each frantic beat echoing in his ears. Hawthorne jerked his legs, desperate for freedom, but encountered the same unyielding bonds. The rush of adrenaline cut through the fog of pain, sharpening his senses even as fear clawed at his insides.

"Hello?" he called out, his voice a hoarse rasp that barely carried. "Is anyone there? What's going on?"

Silence answered him, broken only by the sound of his own ragged breathing. Hawthorne forced himself to inhale deeply, trying to quell the rising tide of panic. Think. You're a federal judge. You've faced down hardened criminals. Use that mind of yours.

He flexed his fingers, feeling the coarse grain of wood beneath them. A chair, then. Wooden, solid. The air was too still, the silence too complete. No traffic sounds, no hum of air conditioning. Underground? Or heavily insulated?

"Whoever you are," Hawthorne said, injecting as much authority into his voice as he could muster, "you've made a grave mistake. I'm a federal judge. There will be people looking for me. Release me now, and we can discuss this rationally."

The words echoed in the emptiness, fading away with no response. Hawthorne's jaw clenched, frustration warring with fear. He was used to being in control, to having his words carry weight. This helplessness was alien, infuriating.

Think, Richard. What would they want with you? A high-profile case? Blackmail? Revenge?

The possibilities spun through his mind, each more unsettling than the last. Whatever the reason, Hawthorne knew one thing with certainty – he needed to find a way out of this nightmare, and fast.

As Hawthorne's eyes strained against the darkness, a faint glow began to seep into his vision. Shadows coalesced into vague shapes, teasing his senses with half-formed silhouettes. Walls materialized around him, their surfaces rough and uneven. A raised platform loomed ahead, its edges softened by the dim light. Rows of seats stretched out before him, their outlines blurring together like a sinister audience.

"What in God's name..." Hawthorne muttered, his judicial composure slipping as recognition dawned.

It was a courtroom. Or at least, it was meant to be. The realization hit him with the force of a gavel strike, sending a chill down his spine. This was his domain, twisted into something unrecognizable and deeply wrong.

As his vision adjusted, the illusion began to crumble. The judge's bench towered above, but its wood grain was too perfect, too flat. Painted, he realized with growing unease. His gaze darted to the gallery chairs, rigid and unnatural, their backs bent at impossible angles. Cardboard, perhaps? Or some cheap facsimile?

Hawthorne strained against his restraints, twisting his head to take in more of this bizarre tableau. "This can't be real," he thought, his mind reeling. "What kind of sick game is this?"

The jury box caught his attention next, its seats empty yet somehow expectant. The prosecution and defense tables stood silent sentinels, devoid of life or purpose. Everything was an artificial, lifeless replica of the chambers he knew so well.

His eyes fell upon the American flag in the corner, and a wave of revulsion washed over him. Its fabric hung stiffly, the stripes uneven and hastily drawn. A mockery of justice, of everything he had dedicated his life to upholding.

"Whoever's responsible for this," Hawthorne called out, his voice echoing in the eerie stillness, "you're making a grave mistake. This... this travesty won't go unpunished."

But even as the words left his mouth, doubt gnawed at him. Who would go to such lengths to recreate a courtroom? And for what purpose? The implications were too disturbing to contemplate.

The hairs on the back of Hawthorne's neck stood on end, a primal warning that sent a chill down his spine. In the oppressive silence of the fake courtroom, a new sound emerged—low and crackling, like an ancient speaker sputtering to life. His muscles tensed, every nerve on high alert.

A voice, distorted and mechanical, echoed from somewhere above him. "Richard Hawthorne, you have been found guilty."

The words dropped into the silence like a stone into deep water, rippling through the artificial courtroom. Hawthorne stiffened, his breath coming faster now, shallow and uneven. Guilty? The very concept seemed to mock everything he stood for.

He swallowed hard, his throat raw and parched. "Guilty of what?" His voice came out hoarse and cracked, barely recognizable as his own. The words hung in the air, unanswered.

Hawthorne's thoughts whirled like a maelstrom. Had one of his rulings come back to haunt him? Was this revenge for some perceived injustice? Or was it something deeper, more personal?

"Answer me!" he demanded, straining against his bonds. "What am I accused of? I have the right to know the charges against me!"

The silence stretched on, oppressive and heavy. Hawthorne's heart hammered in his chest, each beat echoing in the stillness of the artificial courtroom. The faint hum of unseen machinery filled the air, a constant reminder of the surreal nature of his predicament. Something creaked in the shadows, and Hawthorne's head snapped towards the sound, eyes straining in the dim light.

"But," the mechanical voice finally continued, each word slow and deliberate, "you will have a chance to save your own life."

Hawthorne's breath caught in his throat. Save his life? The implication sent a chill down his spine. This was more than a simple kidnapping or act of revenge. This was life or death.

"What do you mean?" he demanded, fighting to keep his voice steady. "What kind of chance?"

The voice didn't respond immediately, leaving Hawthorne to grapple with the weight of his situation. His mind raced, years of legal experience kicking into high gear. This was a trial, yes, but not one governed by any law he recognized. A test, then? But of what?

"Explain yourself!" Hawthorne shouted, frustration and fear bleeding into his tone. "You can't just—"

"Silence," the voice cut him off, its mechanical timbre somehow more menacing than before. "You will speak when spoken to, Judge Hawthorne. Or have you forgotten the rules of your own courtroom?"

Hawthorne clenched his fists, nails digging into his palms. The sting of pain helped ground him, clearing his thoughts. This was a trap, he realized. Every word, every reaction was being judged. But by whom? And to what end?

As the silence descended once more, Hawthorne forced himself to take slow, measured breaths. He couldn't see his judge or jury, but he could feel their presence, watching from the shadows. One thing was painfully clear: the verdict had already been decided. Whatever game this was, whatever sick form of justice his captor sought, Hawthorne knew he was already considered guilty.

He closed his eyes, steeling himself for what was to come. Years on the bench had taught him to remain impartial, to weigh evidence carefully before passing judgment. Now, he found himself on the other side, facing an unseen arbiter who seemed to have no interest in fairness or due process.

"Very well," Hawthorne said, his voice low but steady. "I'm listening. What is this chance you're offering?"

CHAPTER ONE

Special Agent Morgan Cross had been certain her father had died while she was in prison, serving a ten-year-long sentence for a crime she never committed.

And yet as she stood in her living room, with her partner Derik Greene at her side and her Pitbull, Skunk, staring up at her with his big brown eyes, there was no mistaking the voice on the other end of the line.

“Dad?" Her voice was barely above a whisper.

The response made her blood run cold. A voice she thought she'd never hear again. A voice that belonged to a ghost.

"Morgan, it's me."

Her knees buckled, and she gripped the back of the couch for support. Beside her, Derik's brow furrowed with concern. At her feet, Skunk's ears perked up, sensing the sudden tension in the air.

"Dad…" The word felt foreign on her tongue, laced with disbelief and a hint of anger. "How... is this really you?"

"Yes, sweetheart. It's me." His voice was gruff, older, but unmistakably his.

Morgan's mind raced, a torrent of emotions threatening to overwhelm her. How could this be possible? She had mourned him, carried the weight of his loss. And now, here he was, speaking to her as if no time had passed at all.

"I don't understand," she managed, her free hand clenching into a fist. "How can you be alive?"

There was a pause on the other end of the line, filled with the weight of unspoken truths. "It's complicated, Morgan. I can't explain everything over the phone. But I need you to trust me."

Trust. The word echoed in her mind, bitter and sharp. How could she trust a man who had let her believe he was dead? She'd gotten out of prison barely a year ago and had been living under the impression that her father was dead. And since then, she'd been through hell. After getting out of prison, Morgan uncovered a conspiracy within the FBI—a conspiracy that had involved Richard Cordell, a former high-ranking member of the FBI, taking part in framing Morgan. She'd found out that it had all linked back to her father, who had hidden his own identity as an FBI agent from her. But her father had been dead. Morgan had been navigating this alone… and yet here was her father.

Derik moved closer, his hand coming to rest on her shoulder. Right—Morgan hadn't been fully alone. She'd had Derik. She could feel the question in his touch, see the worry etched on his face. But she couldn't bring herself to meet his eyes. Not now, when her world was crumbling around her.

"Why now?" she asked, her voice stronger now, edged with the steel that had kept her going through years in prison and the relentless pursuit of justice afterward. "Why come back after all this time?"

Her father sighed, a sound heavy with regret and something else... fear? "Because you're in danger, Morgan. And I can't live anymore knowing I haven't told you the truth."

The words hung in the air, ominous and foreboding. Morgan's grip on the phone tightened, her knuckles turning white. She thought of Richard Cordell, of the corruption that ran deep in the FBI, of Thomas's death. Thomas Grady—the man whom she'd found out may be her half-brother. Another secret, hidden by her father. How much did her father know? How long had he been watching from the shadows?

"So tell me now," she pressed, her investigator's instincts kicking in despite the emotional turmoil.

"I can't say more now. It's not safe." There was urgency in his voicc now. "Morgan, I know you have questions. I know you're angry. But right now, I need you to listen to me."

She closed her eyes, fighting back the tears that threatened to spill. Skunk whined softly, pressing his head against her leg in a gesture of comfort. She reached down absently to scratch behind his ears, grateful for the familiar touch.

"I'm listening," she said finally, her voice barely audible.

"I'm sorry, Morgan. I should have reached out sooner, but I had my doubts. Now, I need you to come back to the woods—alone. Make sure you're not followed."

She could barely process his words, her mind reeling. The tattoos on her arms seemed to writhe with her inner turmoil. "Dad, I can't just—"

"It's crucial," he cut her off, his voice edged with urgency. "Your safety depends on it."

Morgan's gaze flicked to Derik, his green eyes filled with concern. She couldn't fathom facing this without him. "I'm not going without Derik," she insisted, her voice stronger than she felt.

"No," her father's response was immediate and firm. "It's too dangerous. You must come alone, Morgan. Please."

The desperation in his tone sent a chill down her spine. Derik, reading the conflict on her face, shook his head silently. His jaw was set, worry lines creasing his forehead. Morgan knew he was thinking of the last time they were separated, of the betrayal that had nearly torn them apart.

But this was her father. The man she'd mourned, whose loss had left a void in her life. She had to know the truth.

"Okay," she said finally, her voice barely above a whisper. "I'll come. Tonight."

"Thank you," her father's relief was palpable. "I'll explain everything when you get here. Be careful, Morgan."

As the call ended, Morgan lowered the phone, feeling as if she'd just agreed to step off a cliff. Derik's disapproval radiated from him in waves, but she couldn't meet his eyes. Instead, she knelt down to Skunk, burying her face in his fur, seeking comfort in his unwavering loyalty.

"I have to do this," she murmured, more to herself than to Derik or the dog. The weight of her decision settled on her shoulders.

Morgan stood, her fingers still tangled in Skunk's fur. She finally met Derik's gaze, bracing herself for the inevitable confrontation.

"This is insane, Morgan," Derik burst out, his green eyes flashing with a mixture of concern and frustration. "It could be a trap. Hell, it probably is a trap. You don't know who's really on the other end of that call."

"It was him, Derik," Morgan insisted, her voice low but firm. "I'd know my father's voice anywhere."

Derik ran a hand through his slicked-back hair, mussing it in his agitation. "Even if it is him, why now? It doesn't add up. He already stood you up in the woods when you went after he wrote that letter."

Morgan's jaw clenched. "That's exactly why I have to go. To get answers."

"At least let me come with you," Derik pleaded, taking a step towards her. "We're partners, remember?"

The word 'partners' hung in the air between them, laden with meaning beyond their professional relationship. Morgan's heart clenched, remembering the betrayal that had once threatened to destroy their bond. But she also remembered the forgiveness, the trust they'd rebuilt.

"I can't," she said softly. "He was clear about that. But I won't be alone." She glanced down at Skunk, who sat alertly at her feet, his muscular body taut with readiness. "Skunk will be with me."

***

The headlights of Morgan's SUV cut through the darkness, illuminating a narrow strip of asphalt that stretched endlessly before her. Her knuckles were white on the steering wheel as she pushed deeper into the countryside, leaving the familiar lights of Dallas far behind.

"What do you think, Skunk?" Morgan asked, glancing at the rearview mirror where her loyal pitbull sat attentively in the backseat. "Are we walking into a trap, or am I about to see a ghost?"

Skunk's ears perked up at the sound of her voice, but he offered no answers. Morgan sighed, her mind racing with possibilities.

As the miles ticked by, the landscape began to change. The open fields gave way to dense forests, the trees looming closer to the road with each passing minute. Shadows deepened, and Morgan felt a familiar tightness in her chest.

"It's like stepping back in time," she murmured, memories flooding her mind unbidden.

She could almost smell the crisp autumn air from her childhood, hear her father's deep laugh as they trudged through these very woods. The weight of her first hunting rifle in her hands, the pride in her father's eyes as she took careful aim.

But then, another memory surfaced – sharp, painful. The crack of a branch, a moment of imbalance, and then searing pain as her ankle twisted beneath her.

"Dammit," Morgan hissed, shaking her head to clear the vivid recollection. She absently rubbed her ankle, the old injury a phantom ache. "What am I doing out here, Skunk?" she asked, her voice barely above a whisper. "Chasing ghosts and half-baked theories?"

But deep down, she knew why. The possibility of answers, of finally understanding the web of lies and deceit that had defined the last decade of her life, was too tantalizing to ignore.

As she neared the familiar stretch of forest, Morgan's heart rate quickened. She pulled off the road, gravel crunching beneath the tires as she brought the SUV to a stop.

For a long moment, she sat there, engine idling, staring into the darkness beyond her headlights. Then, with a deep breath, she killed the engine.

The night enveloped Morgan as she stepped out of the car, a cacophony of forest sounds assaulting her senses. Leaves rustled overhead, their whispers carried on a chilly breeze that nipped at her exposed skin. In the distance, an owl's mournful call pierced the air, sending a shiver down her spine.

Skunk's nails clicked against the gravel as he hopped out behind her, his muscular frame a comforting presence at her side. Morgan's hand instinctively found the grip of her holstered gun, its weight both reassuring and ominous.

"Stay close, boy," she murmured, clicking on her flashlight. The beam cut through the darkness, illuminating a narrow path into the woods.

With each step forward, the knot in Morgan's stomach tightened. The forest seemed to close in around her, unchanged yet somehow different. Memories lurked in every shadow, questions hung heavy in the air like mist.

"I don't like this," she whispered to Skunk, who looked up at her with attentive eyes. "It feels... wrong. Like we're walking into something we can't undo."

The pitbull's only response was a soft whine, but it was enough to keep Morgan moving forward. Her free hand absently stroked his broad head as they picked their way through the underbrush.

"What if it's really him, Skunk?" Morgan's voice cracked slightly. "What if he's been alive all this time? How do I even begin to process that?"

The trees seemed to lean in, as if listening to her doubts. Morgan pushed on, her mind racing with possibilities, each more unsettling than the last. What could have driven her father into hiding? What danger was so great that he'd let his own daughter believe he was dead?

After what felt like an eternity of trekking through the dense forest, Morgan reached a familiar clearing. Her breath caught in her throat as recognition washed over her. This was the spot where she had fallen all those years ago, where her childhood innocence had shattered along with her ankle.

She stopped, her flashlight beam sweeping the area. The world around her fell silent, save for the rhythmic sound of Skunk's breathing beside her. Morgan strained her ears, listening for any sign of her father's presence.

"Dad?" she called out softly, her voice barely above a whisper. "Are you here?"

The forest remained stubbornly quiet, offering no answers to her plea. Morgan's grip tightened on her flashlight, her other hand hovering near her holstered weapon. The silence stretched on, punctuated only by Skunk's steady panting and the pounding of her own heart in her ears.

Then—

A flicker of light caught Morgan's eye, drawing her attention to the far edge of the clearing. Her heart leapt into her throat as she saw a flashlight beam dancing between the trees, growing steadily brighter. Someone was approaching.

"Dad?" she called out again, louder this time, her voice trembling with a mix of hope and apprehension.

The light swung in her direction, momentarily blinding her. Morgan shielded her eyes, squinting against the glare. As the beam lowered, a figure emerged from the shadows, and Morgan's breath caught in her chest.

There he stood, barely ten feet away—her father, a man she'd believed dead. Morgan's flashlight beam settled on his face, illuminating features both familiar and foreign. It was him, undoubtedly, but time had left its mark. His once-dark hair was now streaked with gray, and a thick, unruly beard covered the lower half of his face. Deep lines etched his forehead and the corners of his eyes, speaking of years of hardship and worry.

"Morgan," he said, his voice rough with emotion.

She stared at him, frozen in place, her mind reeling. He looked leaner, almost gaunt, his clothes worn and ill-fitting. This was not the strong, confident man from her memories, but rather someone who seemed to have been running for a very long time.

"Is it really you?" Morgan managed to choke out, her voice barely above a whisper. She wanted to rush forward, to touch him, to make sure he was real and not some cruel apparition conjured by her desperate mind. But caution held her back. "How... how is this possible?"

Her father took a hesitant step forward, his hands raised slightly as if to show he meant no harm. "I know you must have a thousand questions, Morgan. I promise I'll explain everything. But we can't stay here."

Morgan's restraint crumbled. In three swift strides, she closed the distance between them and threw her arms around her father. The familiar scent of pine and leather enveloped her, triggering a flood of childhood memories. She clung to him, her fingers digging into the worn fabric of his jacket, as if afraid he might disappear again if she let go.

"Dad," she choked out, her voice muffled against his chest. Tears stung her eyes, blurring her vision. The reality of his presence overwhelmed her senses. He was here, alive, his heart beating steadily against her cheek.

John's arms wrapped around her, hesitant at first, then tightening as he pulled her close. "I'm sorry, Morgan," he whispered, his voice thick with emotion. "I'm so sorry."

For a moment, Morgan allowed herself to be that little girl again, safe in her father's embrace. But as the initial shock began to wear off, a simmering anger rose within her. She pulled back, her hands still gripping his arms, and searched his weathered face.

"Why?" she demanded, her voice quavering with a mix of fury and hurt. "Why did you let me believe you were dead? Do you have any idea what I've been through?"

John's eyes, so like her own, were filled with pain and regret. "Morgan, I--"

"No," she cut him off, her voice rising. "I mourned you. And all this time..." She released him abruptly, taking a step back. Her hand unconsciously moved to her holstered weapon, a habit born from years of distrust. "Why now? Why reach out after all this time?"

Her father's gaze flickered to her hand, noting the gesture. He sighed heavily, his shoulders sagging. "It's complicated, Morgan. There are things you don't know, dangers I've been trying to protect you from."

Morgan barked out a harsh laugh. "I know more now, Dad. I know about Cordell. I know about Thomas Grady."

The words hung in the air between them, heavy with years of unspoken pain and resentment. Morgan tried to reconcile the man before her with the father she thought she'd lost. She wanted answers, needed them desperately, but a part of her was terrified of what those answers might reveal.

John's eyes darted around the clearing, his posture tense. "We can't talk here," he said, his voice low and urgent. "Come back to my cabin. I'll explain everything once we're safe."

Morgan's jaw clenched, frustration bubbling up inside her. She'd waited too long for answers, and now he wanted her to wait even longer. Her gaze swept over him, taking in the weathered lines of his face, the haunted look in his eyes. This man was both familiar and a stranger.

"Safe from what?" she pressed.

John shook his head, glancing over his shoulder. "Please, Morgan. I promise I'll tell you everything, but not here."

She hesitated, searching his face for any hint of deception. The tightness around his eyes, the slight tremor in his hands – these were signs of genuine fear, not the tells of a liar. Still, after everything she'd been through, trust didn't come easily.

"How do I know this isn't some elaborate trap?" she asked, her voice barely above a whisper. "How do I know you're really... you?"

A sad smile flickered across John's face. "You were wearing your lucky Rangers cap the day you broke your ankle. You insisted I carry you all the way back to the truck, even though I offered to go get help. You said, 'Cross women don't need to be rescued.'"

The memory hit Morgan like a physical blow. She could almost feel the weight of that cap on her head, smell the crisp autumn air. It was a detail so specific, so personal, that it couldn't have been faked.

She swallowed hard, her resolve wavering. Every instinct honed by years in the Bureau screamed at her to be cautious, to demand more information before agreeing to anything. But the part of her that was still that stubborn little girl in the woods, the part that had never stopped missing her father, made the decision for her.

"Okay," Morgan said finally, giving a small nod. "Lead the way."

As they started moving through the darkened forest, Morgan's mind raced. What had her father gotten himself into? How did it connect to her own framing and imprisonment? And most importantly, could she trust the man walking beside her, or was she walking into yet another betrayal?

CHAPTER TWO

The dense canopy of oak and pine cast long shadows across the forest floor, their branches intertwining overhead like gnarled fingers. Morgan's heart hammered against her ribcage as she followed the ghostly figure of her father through the night-shrouded woods. Every snap of a twig beneath her boots sent a jolt of adrenaline coursing through her veins.

Skunk padded silently beside her, his muscular body taut with tension. The pit bull's ears were pricked forward, alert to every rustle in the underbrush. Morgan glanced down at her faithful companion, noting the way his nose twitched rapidly, sampling the air. She'd never seen him this on edge before, not even during their most dangerous cases with the Bureau.

"What is it, boy?" she murmured, her voice barely above a whisper. "What's got you so worked up?"

Skunk's only response was a low whine, his dark eyes fixed on the path ahead. Morgan's unease deepened, settling like a cold stone in the pit of her stomach. She'd learned to trust Skunk's instincts over the years, both before her imprisonment and after. If something had the dog this unsettled, it couldn't be good.

Her father's silhouette moved steadily ahead, weaving between the trees with the ease of long familiarity. Morgan studied his gait, the set of his shoulders. It was him, she was certain of it now. The shock of seeing him alive, after all this time of believing him dead, still hadn't fully sunk in.

"How much further?" she called out, her voice tight with a mixture of anticipation and dread.

Her father half-turned, his features still obscured by shadow. "Not far now," he replied, his gruff tone carrying hints of the man she remembered from childhood. "Just over this next rise."

As they crested the small hill, Morgan caught her first glimpse of the cabin. Nestled in a small clearing, it was barely more than a shack—a dilapidated structure that seemed to sag beneath the weight of time and neglect. Its weathered boards were gray with age, the small windows clouded and lifeless.

"This is where you've been living?" Morgan asked, unable to keep the disbelief from her voice.

Her father grunted in affirmation as he approached the cabin's warped door. "It's not much," he admitted, "but it's kept me hidden. And that's what matters."

As they drew closer, the smell hit her—a potent mixture of woodsmoke, damp earth, and something deeper, mustier. The scent of a life lived in isolation, cut off from the world. Morgan's throat tightened as she took in the stark reality of her father's existence.

The interior of the cabin was no less austere. A single bed occupied one corner, its thin mattress showing the imprint of a solitary sleeper. A rickety table stood nearby, its surface scarred and stained. Against the far wall, a rusting stove hunkered like a forgotten sentinel.

But it was the bookshelf that caught Morgan's eye. Leaning precariously against the wall, its shelves bowed under the weight of their sparse contents. A handful of dog-eared novels, their spines cracked and faded. An old radio, its dial frozen in place. And stacks upon stacks of newspaper clippings, their edges yellowed with age.

This was more than just a hideout. This was a command center of sorts, a place where her father had been... what? Monitoring the outside world? Tracking something? Or someone?

"I know you have questions," her father said, breaking the tense silence. "God knows I owe you answers."

Morgan turned to face him, her arms folded tightly across her chest. The flickering light from the oil lamp he'd lit cast deep shadows across his weathered features. She searched his face, looking for traces of the man she'd known, the father she'd mourned.

"Questions?" she repeated, a bitter laugh escaping her lips. "That's putting it mildly, don't you think? I've spent months thinking you were dead. Months piecing together fragments of the truth. And now..." She gestured around the cabin, her tattooed arms a stark contrast to the drab surroundings. "Now I find out you've been here all along. Hiding. Watching. While I rotted in prison for a crime I didn't commit."

Her father's eyes, so like her own, filled with a pain that seemed to age him even further. "Morgan," he began, his voice rough with emotion. "I never wanted—"

But Morgan cut him off, unwilling to hear excuses. Not yet. Not when the wound of betrayal felt so fresh. "I need answers," she said firmly. "Real answers. About everything. I know your name isn't Christopher Cross," Morgan said, her voice steady despite the tempest of emotions roiling within her. "It's John Christopher. And I know you used to be an FBI agent."

Her father's eyes widened slightly, a flicker of surprise crossing his features before he schooled them back into careful neutrality. Morgan pressed on, drawing on every ounce of her investigative experience to keep her voice level.

"What I don't know is why. Why the lies? Why did you disappear? Why did you let me believe you were dead all this time?"

John sighed heavily, running a calloused hand over his beard. "It's... complicated, Morgan. There are things I've done, things I was involved in... I thought I was protecting you by staying away."

Morgan felt a surge of anger, hot and familiar. "Protecting me?" she scoffed. "I spent ten years in prison, only for you to 'die' just before my release. Do you know how devastated I was"?"

"I know, and I'm sorry." John's piercing gaze bore into Morgan, his eyes searching her face as if trying to gauge how much she truly knew. The silence stretched between them, thick with unspoken truths and long-buried secrets. "What else do you know?" he finally asked, his voice rough with apprehension.

Morgan met his stare unflinchingly, her jaw set with determination. "I've met Richard Cordell," she said, her voice steady despite the turmoil churning inside her. "I know about Mary Price. And her son."

The words hung in the air, heavy with unspoken meaning. Morgan watched as her father's weathered face transformed, shock and pain etching deep lines around his eyes. She could almost see the weight of the past settling onto his broad shoulders.

John's expression hardened, a mask slipping into place, but Morgan caught a glimpse of something else beneath it—raw, unguarded anguish. It was a look she recognized all too well, having seen it in her own reflection countless times during her years behind bars.

Pressing her advantage, Morgan continued, her voice dropping to barely above a whisper. "I watched Thomas Grady get shot in front of me. I saw him die on that pier."

The cabin seemed to shrink around them, the shadows deepening in the corners. Morgan's heart pounded in her chest, each beat a reminder of the moment she'd witnessed Thomas's life slip away. She could still smell the salt air, still feel the rough wood of the pier beneath her feet.

John's entire body went rigid at the mention of Mary Price. He looked away, jaw clenched, as though he was absorbing a blow he should have seen coming. His shoulders slumped slightly, the weight of the past pressing down on him. When he finally spoke, his voice was rough, barely above a whisper.

"Then you know who Thomas really was."

It wasn't a question, but Morgan nodded anyway, her throat tight. "He was my half-brother, wasn't he?"

The words hung in the air between them, heavy with unspoken truths and long-buried secrets. Morgan watched her father intently, noting every micro-expression that flickered across his weathered face. The tightening around his eyes, the slight tremble in his hands - she cataloged it all, her FBI training kicking in even as her emotions threatened to overwhelm her.

For a long moment, her father didn't answer. The silence stretched thin, filled only by the soft crackle of the oil lamp and the distant hoot of an owl outside. Finally, he exhaled a long, shuddering breath that seemed to carry the weight of decades.

"Yes."

That single word, so quietly spoken, hit Morgan like a physical blow. She'd already suspected, had pieced together enough of the puzzle to guess at the truth. But hearing it confirmed, here in this dilapidated cabin with the father she'd thought dead for so long, sent a shiver down her spine.

Morgan replayed every interaction she'd had with Thomas. The initial distrust, the reluctant alliance, the growing sense of connection she'd felt but couldn't explain. It all made a terrible kind of sense now.

"Why didn't you tell me?" she asked, her voice barely audible. "All those years, Dad. You could have said something."

John's eyes, when they met hers, were filled with a pain so deep it made her chest ache. "I thought I was protecting you," he said. "I thought... if you never knew, if I could keep that part of my past buried, you'd be safe."

Morgan let out a bitter laugh. "Safe? I spent ten years in prison. I watched my apparent brother die right in front of me. How exactly did your silence keep me safe?"

She saw the flinch, saw how her words cut him to the quick. But the anger that had been simmering inside her for so long wouldn't be contained. Not now, not when she was finally getting the answers she'd sought for so long.

John sat down heavily on the edge of the bed, the ancient springs creaking under his weight. His weathered hands gripped the frayed edges of the threadbare blanket, knuckles white with tension. Morgan watched as he stared at the worn wooden floor, his eyes unfocused, lost in memories she could only imagine.

"Mary Price," he began, his voice rough with emotion. "She was... everything to me, Morgan. Beautiful, brilliant, fierce." A ghost of a smile played across his lips before fading. "But she wasn't mine. Not really."

Morgan's jaw clenched. "Cordell," she said, the name tasting bitter on her tongue.

John nodded, his expression darkening. "Richard was obsessed with her. Called her his muse, his inspiration. But it was more than that. He saw her as a possession."

The air in the cabin felt thick, oppressive. Morgan's skin crawled at the thought of Cordell's fixation. She'd seen glimpses of his ruthlessness, but this... this was something darker.

"Mary and I," John continued, "we kept everything secret. Stolen moments, whispered promises. We thought we were being careful."

Morgan pieced together the fragments of a past she'd never known. "But he found out," she said, her voice barely above a whisper.

John's eyes met hers, filled with a pain that seemed to stretch across decades. "Yes," he replied. "And when he did..."

The unfinished sentence hung in the air between them, heavy with implications. Morgan's fists clenched at her sides, her nails digging into her palms. She could feel the rage building inside her, a familiar companion after all these years.

"What did he do?" she asked, dreading the answer but needing to hear it.

John's gaze dropped back to the floor. "He wanted revenge, Morgan. On both of us. But Mary... she bore the brunt of his wrath." John's voice turned hollow, echoing in the small cabin like a ghost from the past. "Cordell had Mary killed," he said, the words dropping like stones in still water. "Then he framed me for it."

Morgan's breath caught in her throat. She'd suspected as much, but hearing it confirmed sent a chill through her body. Her tattooed arms wrapped around herself, seeking warmth that wouldn't come.

"How?" she managed to ask, her voice barely audible over the crackle of the oil lamp.

John's weathered hands trembled as he spoke. "He staged it to look like an accident. Cross-fire on a case." His eyes, clouded with memories, met Morgan's. "But I knew. And he knew that I knew."

Morgan connected dots she'd never seen before. "Your career, your life..."

"Gone," John finished. "In an instant. I had no choice but to vanish. To become a ghost."

The weight of his words settled over Morgan like a shroud. She thought of her childhood, of the isolated cabin where she'd grown up, so similar to this one. The pieces were falling into place with sickening clarity.

"That's why we lived in the woods," she said, her voice thick with realization. "You were hiding. Protecting me."

John nodded, his eyes glistening in the lamplight. "I hoped... I prayed it would be enough to keep you safe. To give you a life free from Cordell's shadow."

Morgan's throat tightened. She thought of her own path, the choices that had led her here. "But I became an FBI agent anyway."

"Yes," John said, a mix of pride and fear in his voice. "Following in my footsteps, even though you didn't know it. I was so proud, Morgan. But also terrified."

"Because the closer I got to the truth..."

"The more danger you were in," John finished. He leaned forward, his voice dropping to a whisper. "And then, somehow, Cordell found out who you were."

Morgan's blood ran cold. "How?" she asked, her mind already racing through possibilities. "How did he find out?"

John shook his head, frustration etched on his face. "I don't know. I've been trying to figure that out. But once he knew..." He trailed off, unable to finish the thought.

Morgan filled in the blanks herself. Once Cordell knew, her fate had been sealed. She'd been marked, just like her father before her.

Morgan's fingers traced the faded tattoos on her arms, a physical reminder of the years stolen from her. The dim light of the oil lamp cast eerie shadows across the cabin's worn walls, mirroring the darkness that had shrouded her past for so long. She exhaled slowly, her mind reeling from the weight of her father's confession.

"All this time, Cordell was pulling the strings," she said. "He's been three steps ahead of me from the start."

John's weathered face creased with guilt. "I'm sorry, Morgan. I thought I was protecting you by staying away, by letting you believe I was dead. I never imagined he'd come after you directly."

Morgan's eyes snapped to her father's. "When did you realize? When did you know it was Cordell behind my imprisonment?"

John's gaze dropped to the floor. "It wasn't until just about a year ago before you were released. I'd been monitoring things from afar, trying to piece together what happened. When I finally connected the dots..." He trailed off, his voice thick with regret.

"And that's when you decided to fake your death. Again." Morgan's tone was sharp, accusatory.

John nodded, his shoulders slumping. "I thought if Cordell believed I was truly gone, he'd leave you alone. I hoped your release would be the end of it."

Morgan laughed bitterly. "Well, that worked out great, didn't it?" She ran a hand through her dark hair, frustration bubbling up inside her. "Do you have any idea what it was like, thinking you were dead all this time? Believing I had no one left?"

"I know," John said softly. "And I'll regret that decision for the rest of my life. But Morgan, you have to understand – Cordell is relentless. He doesn't just destroy his enemies; he obliterates them. I couldn't risk him coming after you again."

Morgan closed her eyes, trying to process the enormity of the situation. Her entire life had been shaped by this vendetta, this decades-long game of cat and mouse. And now, she was caught in the middle of it all.

The flickering lamplight cast long shadows across John's weathered face as he leaned forward, his voice low and urgent. "I saw you on the news, Morgan. Your arrest, the accusations. I knew it had to be Cordell. He's still out there, still pulling strings."

Morgan's jaw clenched, her arms tightening across her chest. The cabin suddenly felt too small, too confining. She paced, the floorboards creaking beneath her feet.

"He's not just after me," she said, her dark eyes meeting her father's. "He's trying to erase everything you were, everything you stood for. It's like he wants to wipe out any trace of John Christopher from the world."

John nodded grimly. "Cordell's always been obsessed with legacy. In his mind, I betrayed him, and now he wants to make sure there's nothing left of me. Not even in you."

Morgan stopped pacing, her mind racing. She'd been right about so much, but the confirmation brought no satisfaction. Only a cold, creeping dread.

"What am I supposed to do?" she asked, hating how lost she sounded. "Cordell's got allies everywhere. He's got his hooks so deep in the Bureau, I don't know who I can trust anymore." She ran a hand through her dark hair, frustration etched in every line of her body. "I'm running out of options, Dad. And I'm running out of time."

John's weathered face darkened, his eyes taking on a haunted look that sent a chill down Morgan's spine. He stepped back, running a calloused hand through his graying hair.

"There might be another way," he said, his voice low and gravelly. "A way to end this once and for all."

Morgan tensed, her FBI instincts screaming a warning. "What are you thinking?"

John met her gaze, his expression grim. "I turn myself in. Surrender to Cordell."

The words hit Morgan like a physical blow. Her blood ran cold, her heart hammering against her ribs. "Absolutely not," she snapped, her voice sharp with fear and anger.

"Think about it," John pressed. "If I give myself up, maybe it'll be enough. Maybe he'll finally let this vendetta go."

Morgan shook her head vehemently, her dark hair whipping around her face. "You don't understand how Cordell operates," she said, her voice tight with urgency. "He doesn't just kill his enemies. He erases them."

She paced the small cabin, her tattooed arms crossed tightly over her chest. Her mind raced, imagining all the ways Cordell could twist this to his advantage. "If you surrender, he won't just kill you," she continued, turning back to face her father. "He'll take someone away from you first. And that someone will be me."

John's face paled, the implications sinking in. Morgan pressed on, her voice softening slightly. "We can't give him that opportunity. You need to stay hidden, Dad. Let me handle this."

"But how?" John asked, his shoulders slumping with the weight of their predicament.

Morgan's jaw set with determination. "I'll find a way to bring Cordell down. For good this time. But I need you safe while I do it."

The oil lamp flickered, casting dancing shadows across the weathered walls of the cabin. Morgan sank onto the edge of the rickety bed, her body heavy with exhaustion and the weight of everything she'd learned. Outside, the forest hummed with nocturnal life, a contrast to the oppressive silence within.

She ran a hand through her dark hair, her mind whirling. The lies, the betrayals, the decades of secrets – it was almost too much to process. But beneath the shock and confusion, a fierce determination burned. This wasn't just about clearing her name anymore. This was war.

"I need to form a plan," Morgan muttered, more to herself than to her father. She glanced up at him, noting the worry lines etched deep into his face. "Cordell has allies everywhere. Taking him down won't be easy."

John nodded gravely. "He's had years to build his network. But you're not alone in this fight, Morgan. Remember that."

A ghost of a smile touched her lips. "I know. I've got good people in my corner." Her thoughts drifted to Derik, and something in her expression must have changed, because her father's eyebrow raised slightly.

"I know this is a lot," he went on, "but maybe you can tell your old man how you're doing outside of all this? You have a life… a man?"

Morgan blinked, caught off guard by the sudden shift. "Yeah… Derik. We're... together now," she admitted, feeling an odd mix of vulnerability and warmth. "It's still new, but it's good. Really good."

A genuine smile spread across John's weathered face. "I'm glad to hear that," he said. "That boy's loved you for a long time, you know. Even back when you two were just partners, I could see it in his eyes."

Morgan felt a flush creep up her neck. "Dad," she protested weakly, but there was no real objection behind it. Instead, she found herself relaxing slightly, allowing herself this moment of normalcy amidst the chaos. "He's been there for me through... everything," she continued, her voice growing quiet. "The framing, the prison time, all of it. Even when I pushed him away, he never gave up on me."

John reached out, gently squeezing her shoulder. "That's what love does, sweetheart. It gives you strength when you need it most."

Morgan nodded, swallowing past the lump in her throat. For a brief moment, she allowed herself to simply be a daughter sitting with her father, sharing a piece of her life. But the weight of their situation pressed in again, and she straightened, her expression hardening with resolve.

"We're going to end this," she said, her voice low and determined. "Cordell, his network, all of it. Whatever it takes."

Morgan let the silence settle between them, a comfortable weight. Her father's presence felt both familiar and strange, like rediscovering a part of herself she'd thought lost forever.

"I should go," Morgan said finally, her voice barely above a whisper. "Derik will be worried, and I need to start planning our next move."

John nodded, rising slowly from his seat on the edge of the bed. Morgan stood as well, her body tense with a mixture of reluctance and urgency.

They faced each other, neither quite sure how to bridge the physical and emotional distance. Then, with a sudden surge of emotion, Morgan stepped forward and wrapped her arms around her father. He stiffened for a moment, surprised, before returning the embrace.

Morgan pressed her face against his shoulder, inhaling the scent of pine and woodsmoke that clung to his clothes. It transported her back to childhood camping trips, to moments of safety and belonging that had seemed lost forever.

"I'm glad you're alive, Dad," she murmured, her voice thick with unshed tears. "I thought... for so long, I thought I'd lost you too."

John's arms tightened around her. "I'm sorry, sweetheart," he said, his own voice rough with emotion. "I never wanted to leave you. But I thought... I thought it was the only way to keep you safe."

Morgan pulled back slightly, meeting her father's gaze. The determination that had driven her for the past decade blazed in her eyes. "We're going to fix this," she said. "Together. No more running, no more hiding. It's time Cordell paid for everything he's done."

John nodded, a mix of pride and concern etched on his weathered features. "Be careful, Morgan. Cordell's dangerous, and he's got a lot of powerful friends."

"I know," Morgan replied, her jaw set. "But so do I. And I've got the truth on my side."

As she turned to leave, Morgan paused at the cabin door, looking back at her father. The enormity of what lay ahead weighed heavily on her shoulders, but for the first time in years, she didn't feel alone in the fight.

"I'll be in touch," she promised. "Stay safe, Dad. We've got a lot of lost time to make up for."

CHAPTER THREE

Golden rays pierced through the gaps in the blinds, painting warm streaks across Morgan's bedroom walls. The tantalizing aroma of coffee and sizzling bacon wafted in, tugging at her senses. For a fleeting moment, as her eyes fluttered open, the world felt deceptively ordinary. Normal. Safe.

But reality crashed over her like a tidal wave, drowning that illusion in an instant. Her father was alive. The thought sent a jolt through her body, and she sat up abruptly, her heart pounding against her ribcage.

"Not now," she muttered, running a hand over her face, feeling the rough edges of scars earned during her time behind bars. She pushed the thought away, but it lingered, persistent as the morning light creeping across her skin.

From the kitchen came the familiar sounds of Derik moving about. The clatter of a frying pan against the stove. The low murmur of the morning news from the small TV. It was all so routine, so mundane—as if the earth-shattering revelations of last night had never happened.

But they had. And now, everything had changed.

Morgan swung her legs over the side of the bed, her bare feet touching the cool hardwood floor. She closed her eyes, trying to center herself, to find some semblance of normalcy in the chaos that had become her life.

"You've faced worse," she reminded herself, her voice barely above a whisper. "Prison. Betrayal. False accusations. This is just another hurdle."

But even as the words left her lips, she knew it was a lie. This was different. This was personal in a way nothing else had been.

She stood, her legs slightly unsteady, and made her way to the bedroom door. As she reached for the handle, she caught sight of her reflection in the mirror. The woman staring back at her was a far cry from the bright-eyed agent she'd once been. Now, her dark eyes held a hardness, a wariness that spoke of years spent looking over her shoulder.

"Time to face the music," she murmured, steeling herself for what lay beyond that door. For the conversation she knew was coming with

Derik. For the reality of a world where her father—a man she'd mourned, a man she'd believed dead—was suddenly, impossibly alive.

With a deep breath, she turned the handle and stepped out into the hallway, the scent of breakfast growing stronger, a mundane anchor in a sea of uncertainty.

Morgan tugged the zipper of her worn FBI Academy hoodie up to her chin as she padded into the kitchen. The familiar aroma of coffee and pancakes wrapped around her like a comforting embrace.

Derik stood at the stove, his broad shoulders tense beneath his white t-shirt as he flipped a pancake with practiced ease. Skunk, ever the opportunist, sat at attention nearby, his brown eyes fixed on Derik's every move, tail thumping hopefully against the linoleum floor.

"Morning," Derik said, his voice low and gravelly. He didn't turn around, didn't elaborate. He didn't have to.

Morgan's throat tightened as she remembered the weight of last night's confession. How she'd poured out the impossible truth about her father, about Cordell, about the web of lies and danger that now ensnared them both. She could see it in the rigid set of Derik's jaw as he slid a plate of golden pancakes in front of her, in the way his green eyes, usually so warm, now held a glimmer of worry.

"Thanks," she murmured, settling onto a bar stool. Her fingers curled around the warm mug of coffee he'd already prepared for her, black with two sugars, just the way she liked it. The familiarity of the gesture made her heart ache.

"Sleep okay?" Derik asked, his tone carefully neutral as he leaned against the counter, his own mug cradled in his hands.

Morgan let out a humorless chuckle. "As well as can be expected when your whole world's been turned upside down."

Derik nodded, a muscle in his cheek twitching. "Morgan, about Cordell-"

"I know what you're going to say," she cut him off, her voice low and intense. "That we should go to the Bureau, that we need backup. But we can't. Not yet. Not until we know who we can trust."

She watched as Derik's knuckles whitened around his mug, saw the conflict play out across his face. "He's dangerous, Morgan. You know that better than anyone."

"Yeah, I do," she agreed, her gaze dropping to the syrup slowly spreading across her untouched pancakes. "But so am I. And I'm not about to let him win. Not after everything he's taken from me."

The silence stretched between them, heavy with unspoken fears and the ghosts of past betrayals. Morgan knew Derik was worried, knew he was struggling with the desire to protect her and the knowledge that she needed to fight this battle on her own terms.

Finally, Derik sighed, setting his mug down with a soft clink. "Just... promise me you won't shut me out again. Whatever happens, whatever you're planning, I want to be there. We're partners, remember?"

Morgan looked up, meeting his gaze. The concern in his eyes made her chest tighten. She reached out, covering his hand with her own. "I promise," she said softly. "We're in this together."

As if sensing the tension, Skunk chose that moment to let out a low whine, his nose nudging Derik's leg. Despite everything, Morgan felt a small smile tug at her lips. "I think someone's feeling left out of the pancake party."

Derik chuckled, the sound warming Morgan more than any cup of coffee could. "Alright, alright," he said, tossing a small piece of pancake to the eager dog. "But don't tell Morgan I'm spoiling you."

For a brief moment, as Skunk happily munched his treat and Derik's hand remained warm beneath her own, Morgan allowed herself to believe that they might just make it through this. That together, they could face whatever Cordell threw their way.

But deep down, she knew the calm wouldn't last. Cordell was out there, waiting, planning. And she had to be ready.

The harsh buzz of her phone shattered the fragile peace, vibrating against the kitchen table with an urgency that made Morgan's stomach clench. She glanced at the caller ID, her jaw tightening. Mueller.

Morgan's hand hovered over the device, her mind racing. Mueller had been an ally, true, but the revelation about her father changed everything. Trust was a luxury she couldn't afford, not with Cordell's shadow looming over them.

She caught Derik's eye, saw the question there, and gave a slight nod. Only he could know the truth. Only he could be trusted completely.

"Cross," she answered, her voice steady despite the rapid beating of her heart.

"Morgan." Mueller's gravelly tone came through, tinged with something she rarely heard from him – urgency. "We've got a situation."

She straightened, instantly on alert. "What kind of situation?"

"Murder," Mueller said bluntly. "High-profile. A federal judge, Richard Hawthorne."

Morgan's breath caught. A judge. This wasn't some run-of-the-mill homicide. This was big.

"How bad?" she asked, though she already suspected the answer.

"Bad enough that they called us in immediately," Mueller replied. "The crime scene... it's unlike anything I've seen. We need you here."

Morgan exhaled slowly, her gaze falling on the untouched plate before her. So much for breakfast. "Text me the address. I'll be there in twenty."

She ended the call, looking up to find Derik already moving, grabbing his jacket. His green eyes met hers, filled with determination and a hint of worry. "I heard enough," he said. "Let's go."

As they headed for the door, Morgan's mind raced. A federal judge murdered, a bizarre crime scene – was this Cordell's work? Or was she seeing ghosts in every shadow now? Either way, she couldn't shake the feeling that this was just the beginning of something much bigger, much darker.

And as they stepped out into the crisp morning air, Morgan steeled herself for whatever horrors awaited them. The game had changed, the stakes raised. But she was ready. She had to be.

***

The stench of decay and neglect assaulted Morgan's senses as she and Derik descended the crumbling concrete steps into the basement. Flickering fluorescent lights cast an eerie, sickly glow on the peeling walls, creating dancing shadows that seemed to mock their presence.

"Jesus," Derik muttered, his hand instinctively moving to the small of his back where his weapon rested. "This place looks like it hasn't seen a living soul in decades."

Morgan's eyes narrowed as she surveyed the scene. "Perfect spot for a murder, though. Isolated, forgotten..." She trailed off, her mind already racing ahead, piecing together the killer's possible motivations.

As they reached the bottom of the stairs, Morgan paused, her nostrils flaring slightly. Beneath the musty odor of mildew and rot, there was something else. Something metallic. Blood.

"You smell that?" she asked Derik, her voice low.

He nodded grimly.

They pushed through a set of rusted double doors, and Morgan felt her breath catch in her throat. The scene before her was so incongruous, so utterly bizarre, that for a moment she wondered if she'd stepped into some twisted funhouse mirror version of reality.

"What the hell?" Derik breathed beside her.

Before them stood a meticulously crafted facsimile of a courtroom. The judge's bench loomed at the far end, flanked by a jury box and witness stand. But this was no place of justice. This was a mockery, a cruel parody built from plywood and cheap veneer.

Morgan tried to process the scene. Why here? Why like this? The symbolism was obvious, almost heavy-handed. But what was the killer trying to say?

"It's like a stage set," she murmured, taking a cautious step forward. Her eyes swept over every detail, cataloging, analyzing. "But who was the audience supposed to be?"

Derik moved beside her, his posture tense. "Just the judge, maybe? Some kind of sick game?"

Morgan nodded slowly, her gaze fixed on the empty judge's chair. "Yeah. A game where the stakes were life and death." She turned to Derik, her expression grim. "And our victim lost."

As they moved deeper into the mock courtroom, Morgan couldn't shake the feeling that they were being watched. Not by the killer – he was long gone – but by something else. The weight of judgement, perhaps. Or the ghosts of injustices past.

Morgan's pulse quickened as her eyes adjusted to the harsh glare of the forensic lights. The makeshift courtroom, once shrouded in darkness, now revealed its sinister secrets under the unforgiving illumination.

"Jesus," she breathed, her voice barely above a whisper. "It would've been pitch black when they brought him in. Can you imagine? Waking up here, alone in the dark?"

Derik's jaw tightened. "A final judgment."

Morgan nodded, her mind racing. "The victim was the only audience. This whole setup... it was for him."

She took a careful step forward, her trained eyes scanning every inch of the space. As she moved, the hidden details began to emerge, each one more horrifying than the last.

"Watch your step," she warned Derik, her voice tight with tension. "This isn't just a crime scene. It's a death trap."

Before them lay an intricate web of destruction, something pulled straight from a nightmare. Trip wires glinted in the harsh light, stretched taut across the floor. Crude blades hung suspended, poised to strike at the slightest provocation. Every surface seemed rigged with some deadly mechanism, waiting to be triggered.

"It's like a twisted game of Mousetrap," she muttered, crouching to examine a particularly complex contraption. "Whoever did this wanted the victim to trigger his own death."

As she studied the elaborate setup, a nagging thought tugged at the back of her mind. The level of planning, the meticulous attention to detail... it reminded her of something. Or someone.

Morgan turned to Derik, her eyes locking with his. The unspoken understanding passed between them, a silent acknowledgment of the gravity of what they were facing. This wasn't some heat-of-the-moment crime; it was a calculated, meticulously planned execution.

"This is way beyond a typical homicide," Derik murmured, his green eyes scanning the mock courtroom. "The level of detail, the precision..."

Before Morgan could respond, an officer approached, his face grim. "Agents, we've confirmed the victim's identity. It's Federal Judge Richard Hawthorne."

The name hit Morgan like a punch to the gut. She'd heard of Hawthorne - a man known for his tough sentencing and controversial rulings. A man who'd made plenty of enemies over the years.

"A federal judge," Morgan said, her voice low. "Christ, this is going to be a shitstorm."

She couldn't help but think of her own experiences with the justice system, of the years stolen from her by corruption and lies. Had Hawthorne been part of that system? Or was he a target because he'd tried to fight against it?

"This wasn't just a murder," Morgan said, her eyes narrowing as she surveyed the grotesque scene once more. "This was a message. A very loud, very clear message."

Derik nodded, his jaw tightening. "The question is, who was it meant for? And why go to all this trouble?"

Morgan connected dots, searching for patterns. Could this be related to Cordell? To her father? Or was this an entirely new player entering the game?

"I don't know," she admitted, "but I intend to find out."

With a deep breath, Morgan steeled herself and moved towards the lifeless form on the cold concrete floor. Judge Hawthorne lay there, his once-pristine suit now a canvas of blood and violence. He was so close to the exit, mere feet from potential safety. The sight stirred something in Morgan - a mix of pity and a grim determination to uncover the truth.

Morgan crouched beside Judge Hawthorne's body, her tattooed arms braced against her knees. The coppery scent of blood filled her nostrils, mingling with the musty basement air. Her eyes traced the dark trail leading from the makeshift courtroom to where the judge now lay.

"He almost made it," she murmured, more to herself than to Derik. Her gaze fixed on Hawthorne's outstretched hand, fingers curled as if grasping for the door handle just beyond his reach. "Look at his hand, Derik. He was fighting till the end."

Derik stepped closer, his face a mask of concern. "What are you thinking, Morgan?"

She didn't answer immediately, her mind racing. This scene, this elaborate setup – it reminded her of something, but she couldn't quite place it. Her fingers ghosted over the judge's bloodstained sleeve, careful not to disturb any evidence.

"The wound," she said finally, pointing to a jagged tear in Hawthorne's side. "It wasn't immediately fatal. He had time to try and escape."

Morgan's stomach churned as she imagined Hawthorne's final moments. The fear, the desperation, the slow realization that he wouldn't make it.

"Morgan?" Derik's voice pulled her back to the present.

She shook her head, pushing away the memories. "Sorry. It's just... this is sick, Derik. Whoever did this wanted him to suffer."

As she spoke, Morgan's eyes caught on something glinting near the judge's body. Carefully, she leaned in for a closer look. A small, jagged piece of metal lay on the concrete, coated in dried blood.

"There," she said, gesturing for Derik to see. "That's what got him. Part of one of those damn traps."

Morgan stood, her knees protesting after crouching for so long. She surveyed the room again, trying to piece together Hawthorne's final moments.

"He triggered something in that mockery of a courtroom," she mused aloud. "Got hit, but not bad enough to drop him immediately. He made a run for it, almost got out, but..."

"But the blood loss was too much," Derik finished grimly.

Morgan nodded, her jaw clenching. "He bled out here. Alone. Probably calling for help that never came."

Morgan's eyes swept across the macabre scene once more, her mind racing to connect the dots. The fake courtroom, the intricate death traps, the judge's final desperate crawl towards freedom—it all reeked of meticulous planning and a twisted sense of justice.

"This wasn't random," she said, her voice low and tense. "Look at the setup, Derik. The attention to detail. Whoever did this wanted Hawthorne to feel something before he died."

Derik stepped closer, his brow furrowed. "What are you thinking? Guilt? Fear?"

Morgan shook her head, her fingers absently tracing the outline of one of her tattoos through her sleeve. "Maybe. Or revenge. This feels... personal."

She walked the perimeter of the room, her trained eyes cataloging every detail. The cheap wood of the judge's bench, the carefully positioned jury box, even the tattered American flag hanging limply in the corner. It was all a carefully crafted illusion, designed to disorient and terrify.

"They wanted him to know exactly why he was here," Morgan muttered, more to herself than to Derik. "This wasn't just about killing him. It was about making him face something." She turned to face him, her expression grim. "I'm thinking this is just the opening act, Derik. Whoever orchestrated this? They're putting on a show. And I've got a feeling we're all going to be in the audience for what comes next."

The weight of her words hung in the air, mingling with the acrid smell of blood and fear that permeated the room. Morgan's hand instinctively went to her phone, thumb hovering over her father's number. But she hesitated. How much did he know? How much more was there to uncover in this web of corruption and revenge?

One thing was certain: the game had changed. And as Morgan stared at the lifeless body of Judge Hawthorne, she couldn't shake the feeling that she was standing at the precipice of something far bigger and more dangerous than she had ever imagined.

CHAPTER FOUR

The stench of death clung to the photographs spread across the briefing room table. Morgan's eyes burned from hours of staring at the gruesome images, each one a piece of the twisted puzzle laid out before her. Judge Richard Hawthorne's lifeless face stared back at her from glossy eight-by-tens, his eyes wide with the terror of his final moments.

She picked up a photo of the mock courtroom, studying the meticulous attention to detail. Cardboard cutouts of a jury. A judge's bench fashioned from plywood. Even a witness stand, complete with a microphone. The killer had recreated every element with chilling precision.

"This wasn't just a murder," Morgan muttered, her voice rough from lack of sleep. "This was a goddamn performance." Morgan's mind raced, piecing together the killer's methodology. "Why go to all this trouble? Why not just put a bullet in his head and be done with it?"

She stood, pacing the length of the room as she spoke her thoughts aloud. "No, this was personal. Whoever did this wanted Hawthorne to suffer. Wanted him to feel trapped, helpless..."

Her voice trailed off as a chill ran down her spine. The sensation was all too familiar—the same helplessness she'd felt when she was framed, when the cell door slammed shut behind her for a crime she didn't commit.

Morgan shook her head, forcing herself back to the present. "Focus, Cross," she chided herself. "This isn't about you. This is about Hawthorne."

But even as she said it, she couldn't shake the nagging feeling that there was more to this case than met the eye. Was it possible that Cordell was involved? The thought made her blood run cold.

She picked up another photo, this one showing the saw that had impaled Hawthorne. The weapon was crude but effective, designed for maximum pain and suffering. Morgan's stomach turned as she imagined Hawthorne's final moments, desperately trying to escape the trap set for him.

"What did you do, Judge?" she whispered to the photo. "Who did you piss off so badly that they'd go to these lengths?"

Morgan's eyes narrowed as she stared at the crime scene photo, her tattooed fingers tracing the outline of the exit door. Something about it didn't sit right with her. She leaned back in her chair, the metal creaking under her weight, and closed her eyes, trying to visualize the scene.

"Why give him an out?" she muttered to herself, her voice barely above a whisper. "It doesn't make sense."

She stood abruptly, pacing the length of the briefing room. Her dark brown hair, pulled back in a tight ponytail, swung with each step.

If I wanted revenge, Morgan thought, her mind racing, *I wouldn't give my target a chance to escape. Unless...*

She paused, her gaze fixed on the far wall but seeing something beyond it. "Unless the escape was part of the game."

Morgan returned to the table, rifling through the reports until she found what she was looking for—the coroner's preliminary findings. She scanned the document, her breath catching as she reached a particular detail.

The cruelty of such a scenario wasn't lost on Morgan. She knew all too well the pain of having hope dangled in front of you, only to have it ripped away. Her own experiences in prison, the years of fighting to clear her name, came flooding back.

Morgan's frown deepened as she stared at the crime scene photos spread across the table. Her fingers traced the outline of Judge Hawthorne's body, mere inches from the exit. The frustration gnawed at her.

"What am I not seeing?" she muttered, her dark eyes scanning the images for the hundredth time. The mock courtroom, the elaborate traps, the carefully orchestrated death—it all spoke of meticulous planning. But that door... that unlocked, unguarded door. It was a discordant note in an otherwise perfectly composed symphony of vengeance. The puzzle pieces were there, but they refused to fit together. Morgan could feel the answer hovering just out of reach, taunting her.

Her concentration was abruptly shattered as the door swung open. Derik strode in, his green eyes bright with a mix of excitement and fatigue. Morgan's heart did a small flip at the sight of him, a reaction she was still getting used to.

"Morgan," he said, slightly out of breath. "We've got something."

She straightened, immediately alert. "What is it?"

"The landlord of the basement property," Derik explained, coming to stand beside her. "He's agreed to meet with us."

***

The sedan's tires crunched over gravel as Morgan guided it down the neglected street. Overgrown trees flanked the road, their branches reaching out like gnarled fingers. Houses, once proud, now sagged under the weight of time and neglect. Morgan's eyes darted from one dilapidated structure to the next, her jaw tightening.

They pulled up to a house that seemed to embody decay. Its paint, once white, had chipped away to reveal weathered wood beneath. The porch sagged precariously, and an ancient pickup truck rusted in the driveway, nature slowly reclaiming it.

"This is it," Derik said, checking the address on his phone.

Morgan killed the engine, her eyes fixed on the house. "Let's hope this guy can give us something useful."

As they approached the front door, Morgan's instincts prickled. Something about this place felt off, like walking into a trap. She'd learned to trust that feeling during her time in prison.

Before they could knock, the door creaked open. A man in his sixties appeared, his face a roadmap of hard years. His eyes, sharp and wary, scanned them both.

"You the feds?" he asked, his voice gravelly.

Morgan nodded, reaching for her badge. "Agent Cross, FBI. This is Agent Greene. We're here about—"

"I know why you're here," the man cut her off. "Name's Greg. Guess you better come in."

As Greg turned to lead them inside, Morgan exchanged a glance with Derik. His slight nod told her he'd picked up on the same unease she felt.

"After you," Morgan said to Derik, allowing him to enter first. It was an old habit from prison—never turn your back on an unknown.

As they crossed the threshold, Morgan couldn't shake the feeling that they were walking into something bigger than a simple landlord interview. The pieces of the puzzle were there, just out of reach. And as she followed Greg into the cluttered living room, she couldn't help but wonder if this lead would bring them closer to the truth—or lead them down another dead end in the twisted game they found themselves in.

Morgan's eyes swept the room, taking in every detail. Stacks of yellowed newspapers teetered precariously on end tables, their headlines long outdated. The faint aroma of stale coffee mingled with pipe smoke, tickling her nostrils. A television droned in the background, its volume low but persistent.

"Nice place," Morgan said, her tone neutral. She'd learned long ago that sometimes the best way to get information was to let people fill the silence themselves.

Greg grunted, settling into a worn armchair. "It's home. Now, what exactly do you want to know?"

Morgan leaned against the wall, her posture casual but her mind razor-sharp. "Tell me about the person who rented your basement space."

The old man's face tightened, his eyes darting to the side. "Not much to tell," Greg said, shrugging. "Never met 'em in person."

Morgan raised an eyebrow. "That's unusual, isn't it? Renting to someone you've never seen?"

Greg's fingers drummed on the arm of his chair. "Look, they paid cash. Left it in unmarked envelopes. Rented for three months, no questions asked. That's all there was to it."

This setup was too perfect, too convenient. It reeked of premeditation, of someone who knew exactly how to cover their tracks. Her jaw clenched as she thought of Judge Hawthorne, of the elaborate death trap he'd been subjected to.

"And you never thought to meet them? To verify who they were?" Morgan pressed, her voice harder now.

Greg's eyes narrowed. "Like I said, they paid. That's all that mattered."

Morgan felt a surge of frustration. She'd been on both sides of an interrogation, and she knew when someone was holding back. But pushing too hard now might shut Greg down completely.

"How did you communicate with them?" she asked, forcing her voice to remain calm.

"Email," Greg replied. "That's it. Just emails about the rent and such."

Morgan nodded slowly, her mind already formulating the next steps. They'd need to trace those emails to see if their killer had left any digital breadcrumbs. But something about this felt off. It was too neat, too easy.

As she opened her mouth to ask another question, a chill ran down her spine. The hairs on the back of her neck stood up, a sensation she'd learned to trust both in prison and as an agent. Something wasn't right here. The room suddenly felt too small, too confined.

Her eyes met Derik's, and she saw the same unease reflected there. They needed to wrap this up, to get out and process what they'd learned. Because Morgan had a sinking feeling that this was just the beginning—and that whoever had orchestrated Judge Hawthorne's murder was far from done.

Greg shifted in his seat, his weathered hands fidgeting with the frayed edge of his plaid shirt. Morgan's keen eyes caught the nervous twitch, the way his gaze darted away from hers.

"Look," he said, his voice gruff with discomfort, "I ain't exactly been rolling in dough lately. Bills keep coming, and the roof ain't gonna fix itself." He gestured vaguely at the ceiling, where water stains spread like dark continents. "When someone offers cash, no questions asked... well, a man in my position don't have the luxury of being picky."

Morgan nodded, her face a mask of understanding. She'd been desperate before, knew the weight of choices made when backed into a corner. But desperation could be exploited, and their killer had known exactly how to take advantage.

"I get it," she said, her voice low and steady. "You needed the money. But those emails might be our only lead. Is there any chance you still have them?"

Greg hesitated, his rheumy eyes flickering towards an ancient desktop computer tucked in the corner of the room. Morgan's pulse quickened. If their perpetrator had been careless, even for a moment...

"I suppose I could pull them up," Greg mumbled, pushing himself to his feet with a groan. "Don't delete much. Never know when you might need something."

As he shuffled towards the computer, Morgan exchanged a glance with Derik. Her partner's expression mirrored her own cautious hope. They'd been chasing shadows for days, and now, finally, a tangible lead.

Greg lowered himself into the creaking office chair, his fingers hovering over the keyboard. Morgan moved closer, careful not to crowd him. The ancient machine whirred to life, the fan kicking up dust that danced in the dim light filtering through grimy windows.

'Come on,' Morgan thought, her fingers unconsciously tracing the outline of a tattoo on her wrist – a reminder of her time behind bars, of the patience she'd learned the hard way. 'Give us something, anything.'

As Greg navigated through his cluttered inbox, Morgan's mind raced ahead. What would they find? A carelessly used personal email? An IP address that could be traced? Or another dead end, another piece in a puzzle that seemed to grow more complex with each passing hour?

She thought of Judge Hawthorne, of the grotesque scene they'd discovered. Of Thomas, gunned down on that pier. Of her father, hidden away in the woods, a ghost from a past she was still trying to unravel. Somewhere in this twisted web of lies and vendettas was the truth – and Morgan was determined to drag it into the light, no matter the cost.

Morgan's eyes narrowed as she scanned the email exchange Greg had pulled up. A flicker of excitement coursed through her veins, but it was quickly tempered by years of hard-earned skepticism. This lead felt... convenient. Too convenient.

"There," Greg pointed, his weathered finger tapping the screen. "That's the address they used."

Morgan leaned in, studying the string of seemingly random letters and numbers. "XJ7Q9R2P@encryptmail.com," she muttered, committing it to memory.

Straightening up, she ran a hand through her dark hair, the familiar weight of her gun at her hip a comforting presence. "Mind if I take a picture of this?" she asked Greg, already reaching for her phone.

He shrugged. "Go ahead. Not like I got anything to hide."

Morgan snapped a few photos. This email could be the key to unraveling the whole case, but something nagged at her.

"Derik," she called over her shoulder, "what do you make of this?"

Her partner appeared at her side, his presence a steadying force. "It's something," he agreed, his voice low. "But..."

"But it feels too easy," Morgan finished, meeting his eyes. She saw her own wariness reflected there.

Turning back to Greg, she asked, "Was there anything else unusual about this rental? Any requests, specifications?"

The old man scratched his chin, thinking. "Not really. Just wanted the basement, paid on time. Quiet tenants, never had any complaints."

Morgan nodded, her jaw tightening. Whoever had orchestrated Hawthorne's murder was meticulous, calculated. They wouldn't leave such an obvious trail unless...

"They're not done," she murmured, more to herself than anyone else. "This is just the beginning."

Derik touched her arm gently. "Morgan?"

She shook her head, pushing aside the growing dread. "We need to get this to the tech team, see if they can trace it. But I've got a feeling we're being led down a very specific path."

As they thanked Greg and headed for the door, Morgan couldn't shake the sensation of being watched. She scanned the overgrown yard, the quiet street beyond. Nothing seemed out of place, and yet...

"What are you thinking?" Derik asked as they climbed into their car.

Morgan's hand hovered over the ignition. "I'm thinking Hawthorne was just the opening act. And whoever's behind this? They're playing a long game."

She started the engine, her mind already racing ahead to their next move. But beneath the determination, a cold certainty settled in her gut. This case was far from over, and the true horror was yet to come.

CHAPTER FIVE

The man's footsteps echoed softly in the cavernous space as he moved with deliberate precision. His eyes, sharp and focused, scanned every detail of his surroundings. The abandoned warehouse loomed around him, a cathedral of rust and decay. Concrete floors stretched out beneath his feet, marred by years of neglect. Exposed pipes snaked along the walls and ceiling, their metal surfaces dulled by time.

Dim overhead lights flickered intermittently, casting elongated shadows that danced and twisted with each movement. The air hung heavy with the musty scent of disuse and the faint metallic tang of his creations.

He paused, tilting his head as if listening for something beyond the oppressive silence. Satisfied, he returned his attention to the task at hand.

"Perfect," he murmured, his voice barely above a whisper. "Everything is coming together exactly as planned."

His fingers trailed along the edge of a metal table, feeling the cool smoothness beneath his touch. Upon it lay an array of tools - each one meticulously cleaned and arranged with surgical precision.

He selected a small wrench, weighing it in his palm for a moment before moving towards the center of the room. There, bathed in a pool of sickly yellow light, stood his masterpiece.

The trap was a symphony of interlocking parts - chains hung from the ceiling in complex patterns, pulleys were mounted at strategic points, and gleaming blades lay concealed within innocuous-looking panels. It was beautiful in its complexity, a delicate balance of physics and engineering.

"You'll be my finest work yet," he said softly, addressing the mechanism as if it were a living thing. "A true test of wit and will."

He knelt down, making a minute adjustment to one of the lower mechanisms. In his mind, he could already see it in action - the fluid motion of metal against metal, the inevitable outcome when flesh met steel.

Will they be clever enough to see the solution? he wondered. *Or will they falter, stumbling blindly into their own demise?*

The thought sent a thrill of anticipation through him. This was more than mere killing - it was art, a challenge to the very limits of human ingenuity and survival instinct.

He stood, taking a step back to admire his handiwork. Every piece was in its place, every trigger set with exacting care. One wrong move, one misstep, and the entire apparatus would spring to life.

"Soon," he promised himself, a smile playing at the corners of his mouth. "Very soon, the game will begin."

His eyes swept over the room once more, noting with satisfaction the stark industrial backdrop that would serve as the stage for his next performance. The concrete, the pipes, the oppressive shadows - all of it added to the atmosphere of dread and desperation he sought to create.

In the silence of the abandoned space, surrounded by the fruits of his labor, the man felt a sense of purpose and control that he found nowhere else in life. Here, in this realm of his own creation, he was god and judge, artist and executioner.

And as he made his final preparations, he knew that somewhere in the city, his next unwitting player was going about their day, blissfully unaware of the test that awaited them. The thought filled him with a dark, anticipatory joy.

His hands glided over the setup, fingers tracing the taut tripwire with reverence. Every touch was deliberate, every adjustment minute yet crucial. The hidden trigger beneath his palm responded to the slightest pressure, a testament to its precision.

He crouched, eye-level with the intricate mechanism. This close, he could appreciate every detail - the gleam of metal, the subtle tension in the chains, the razor-sharp edge of concealed blades. It was beautiful in its deadly efficiency.

Standing, he took several measured steps backward, allowing himself a broader view of his creation. The trap sat at the heart of the room, a spider's web of interlinked parts waiting to be triggered.

This wasn't about mere killing - it was so much more. A test of wit, of will, of one's very survival instinct. He was offering a chance, however slim, at redemption through suffering.

"A game," he mused aloud, "but one with the highest stakes."

His eyes swept the space, taking in every detail. The stark concrete, the exposed pipes, the oppressive shadows - all of it perfect. He had chosen this location months ago, renting it under a false name, preparing it meticulously for this very moment.

"Foresight," he told himself, "is everything."

He circled the room once more, mind racing with possibilities. Would his next player rise to the challenge? Or would they falter, becoming just another nameless victim? The anticipation was intoxicating.

With gloved hands, he meticulously wiped down every surface, erasing any trace of his presence. The soft squeak of the cloth against metal and concrete was the only sound in the cavernous space. He worked methodically, his movements precise and unhurried.

"Patience," he murmured to himself, "is the mark of a true artist."

Even as excitement coursed through his veins, he remained disciplined. Each swipe of the cloth was deliberate, each area checked and rechecked. He couldn't afford a single mistake, a stray fingerprint or overlooked hair. The thrill of the impending game warred with his innate caution.

"Control," he reminded himself. "Always in control."

He paused, surveying his handiwork. The room was immaculate, as if untouched by human hands. A smile tugged at the corners of his mouth, pride swelling in his chest.

"Perfect," he breathed. "As it should be."

His gaze swept over the trap once more, admiring its intricate design. Soon, it would spring to life, testing the limits of human endurance and ingenuity. The thought sent a shiver of anticipation down his spine.

"Are you ready?" he asked the empty air. "Are you worthy of the game?"

He checked his watch, noting the time with satisfaction. Everything was proceeding according to schedule. He was not a man given to impatience or recklessness. Each move was calculated, each moment accounted for.

"The pieces are in place," he mused. "Now, we wait for our player to arrive."

With one final, approving nod, he turned towards the exit. The next phase was about to begin, and he could hardly contain his excitement. But even now, on the cusp of his greatest work yet, he remained composed.

"Let the game," he whispered as he reached for the door, "begin."

CHAPTER SIX

Morgan stood motionless in the dimly lit room, her arms crossed tightly over her chest as she watched the cybercrime specialists work. The glow from multiple computer screens cast an eerie blue light across their focused faces. The rhythmic clicking of keyboards filled the air, punctuated by occasional muttered curses and frustrated sighs.

She fought to keep her expression neutral, but inside, Morgan's mind was running. The anonymous email from the landlord's contact was their best lead so far in Judge Hawthorne's murder. If they could trace it, they might finally have a solid suspect. But as the minutes ticked by, her hope began to fade.

"Anything yet, Carter?" she asked, unable to keep the edge of impatience from her voice.

The lead tech shook his head, not taking his eyes off the screen. "Nothing concrete. This guy's good. Really good."

Morgan's jaw clenched. She thought of Judge Hawthorne, impaled and bleeding out on that basement floor. Of the elaborate death trap he'd been lured into. Whoever had done this was methodical, patient. A ghost who left no traces.

"Keep trying," she said. "There has to be something."

As another half hour crawled by, Morgan paced the small room. Her mind drifted to her father, hiding out in that remote cabin. To Cordell, the puppet master pulling strings from the shadows. She shook her head, forcing herself to focus on the case at hand. One monster at a time.

"Dammit!" Carter slammed his hand on the desk, making Morgan jump. "I'm sorry, Agent Cross. We've tried every decryption method, every filter we have. There's just... nothing."

Morgan's heart sank. She'd known it was a long shot, but part of her had still hoped. "You're sure?"

Carter nodded grimly. "Whoever sent this knew exactly what they were doing. The email's completely untraceable."

Morgan exhaled slowly, tamping down her frustration. "Alright. Thank you for trying. Send me whatever you did manage to find, even if it seems insignificant."

As she turned to leave, one of the younger techs spoke up. "Agent Cross? I know it's not much, but... the level of encryption, the way it was routed? This wasn't some amateur hacker. Whoever did this has serious skills."

Morgan paused in the doorway, considering. "An engineer, maybe?"

The tech shrugged. "Could be. Someone with a deep understanding of systems, for sure."

Morgan nodded, filing away the information. It wasn't much, but it was something. As she stepped into the hallway, her mind was already racing, formulating a new approach. If they couldn't chase the killer directly, they'd have to come at it from another angle.

She pulled out her phone, dialing Derik's number. "Meet me in the briefing room," she said when he answered. "We need to dig into Hawthorne's case history. Specifically, anyone with the skills to pull this off who might have a grudge."

As she hung up, Morgan felt a familiar determination settle over her. The killer might think he was a ghost, but even ghosts cast shadows. And she was going to find his, no matter what it took.

Morgan's jaw clenched as she stared at the array of monitors, each displaying a complex web of dead ends and false trails. The lead cybercrime specialist, a woman with dark-rimmed glasses and perpetually furrowed brows, turned to face her.

"I'm sorry, Agent Cross. This email is a black hole. We've tried every trick in the book and then some, but it's like chasing smoke."

Morgan leaned in, her eyes scanning the intricate diagrams on the screens. "Walk me through it one more time."

The specialist sighed, pointing to various nodes on the display. "The email was bounced through multiple proxy servers across six continents. Each hop was encrypted with a different algorithm. When we finally thought we had a lead, it turned out to be a dummy server in Antarctica, of all places."

"Antarctica?" Morgan's eyebrow raised. "That's... creative."

"Creative and infuriating," the specialist agreed. "Whoever set this up knew exactly what they were doing. They anticipated every standard tracing method and had a counter for each one."

Morgan felt a chill run down her spine, her investigator's instinct kicking into high gear. This wasn't just another case. This was something else entirely.

"So we're dealing with a pro," she muttered, more to herself than anyone else.

The tech nodded grimly. "A pro with resources and time. This level of obfuscation takes planning. Lots of it."

Morgan straightened, crossing her arms tightly across her chest. The pieces were starting to form a picture in her mind, and it wasn't a pretty one.

"This isn't some heat-of-the-moment killer," she said, her voice low and intense. "We're looking at someone who's been plotting this for a long time. Patient. Meticulous."

She turned to the team, her eyes hard with determination. "I want every detail you can give me about the methods used. Even if it seems insignificant. This guy might be good, but nobody's perfect. There has to be a pattern, a signature, something."

As the techs nodded and turned back to their screens, Morgan felt a cold certainty settle in her chest. This case was going to push her to her limits, force her to think in ways she never had before. But she was ready for the challenge.

She watched as one of the senior techs shook his head, a look of defeat on his face. It confirmed what she'd already suspected – they weren't going to crack this through conventional means.

Morgan was already formulating new approaches. If they couldn't track the killer directly, they'd have to come at it from another angle. She needed to dig deeper into Hawthorne's past, find the connection that the killer had so painstakingly tried to erase.

Morgan's phone buzzed in her pocket, its vibration cutting through the tense atmosphere of the cybercrime unit. She fished it out, her heart sinking as she read the message from the forensics team.

"Damn it," she muttered, her fingers tightening around the device.

One of the techs looked up. "Bad news, Agent Cross?"

Morgan nodded, her jaw clenched. "Forensics came up empty. No DNA, no fingerprints, not even a stray hair." She exhaled sharply, frustration etching lines across her forehead. "This guy isn't just good. He's a damn ghost."

She paced the length of the room, her mind racing. The killer had left no digital footprint, no physical evidence. It was as if he'd never existed at all. Morgan could feel the case slipping through her fingers like sand.

"How do we catch someone who doesn't leave a trace?" she wondered aloud, more to herself than anyone else.

The tech shrugged helplessly. "I don't know, Agent. We've tried everything we can think of."

Morgan stopped pacing, her eyes fixed on the monitors displaying dead-end after dead-end. Then, slowly, a new idea began to form.

"Ghosts might not leave traces," she said softly, "but they do leave shadows."

The tech looked at her, confusion evident on his face. "What do you mean?"

Morgan turned to face him, a spark of determination in her eyes. "We've been so focused on chasing the killer, we haven't been looking at the victim closely enough. If we can't track him directly, we need to flip our approach."

She grabbed her jacket from the back of a chair, already heading for the door. "Instead of chasing the killer, we need to focus on Judge Hawthorne. There has to be a connection there, something that made him a target."

As she reached the doorway, Morgan paused, looking back at the team. "Keep digging into that email. Even if you can't trace it, there might be something in the way it's constructed, the language used. Anything that could give us a clue about who we're dealing with."

With that, she strode out of the room, her mind already racing with new possibilities. The killer might be a ghost, but even ghosts had stories. And Morgan was determined to uncover this one, no matter how deeply it was buried.

***

Morgan burst into the briefing room, her eyes immediately locking onto Derik. He was hunched over the table, surrounded by stacks of files, his brow furrowed in concentration.

"Derik," she said, her voice tight with urgency. "We need to change our approach."

He looked up, his eyes questioning. "What do you mean?"

Morgan strode to the table, her fingers drumming against its surface. "Judge Hawthorne. We need to dig into his past cases. All of them."

Derik leaned back in his chair, running a hand through his hair. "That's a lot of ground to cover, Morgan. The judge had a long career."

"I know," she replied, her gaze sweeping over the scattered files. "But it's our best lead right now. We're looking for cases that might have made him a target for revenge."

She began sorting through the files, her movements quick and purposeful. "Violent offenders, Derik. That's what we need to focus on. Criminals who got the book thrown at them by Hawthorne."

Derik nodded, already reaching for a stack of files. "Makes sense. Someone with a grudge, someone who felt wronged by the system."

Morgan paused, her hand hovering over a particularly thick file. "And there's one more thing we need to pay attention to," she said, her voice low. "Release dates."

Derik's eyes widened in understanding. "You're thinking our killer might be someone who just got out?"

"Exactly," Morgan confirmed, her mind racing. "Someone who's had years to plan, to nurture their resentment. And now they're finally free to act on it."

As they settled into their task, Morgan couldn't shake the feeling that they were racing against time. Somewhere out there, a killer was watching, waiting. And she had a sinking feeling that Judge Hawthorne was just the beginning.

Morgan's eyes burned as she pored over yet another case file, the fluorescent lights of the briefing room casting harsh shadows across the scattered papers. Her fingers traced the edge of a particularly worn folder, pausing as a name caught her attention.

"Derik," she called, her voice cutting through the silence. "I think I've got something here."

Her partner looked up from his own stack of documents, eyebrows raised in question. Morgan slid the file across the table, tapping a finger on the name at the top.

"Marcus Walsh," she said, her tone tight with anticipation. "Take a look at this one."

Derik leaned forward, his eyes scanning the page. "Voluntary manslaughter," he murmured, frowning. "Fifteen years ago. What about it?"

Morgan stood, pacing the length of the table as she spoke. "It was a crime of passion. One moment of violence that spiraled out of control. But look at the sentence Hawthorne handed down."

Derik's eyes widened as he found the information. "Fifteen years? That's..."

"Unusually harsh," Morgan finished for him, her mind racing. "The standard for cases like this is typically five to eight years. Hawthorne went well beyond that."

She stopped pacing, bracing her hands on the back of a chair as she met Derik's gaze. "Can you imagine sitting in a cell for fifteen years, knowing you got more than double the usual sentence? That kind of resentment... it could eat away at a person."

Derik nodded slowly, his expression grim. "It's a strong motive, that's for sure. But is it enough to turn someone into... this?" He gestured vaguely, encompassing the horror of the crime scene they'd witnessed.

Morgan sank into the chair, her exhaustion momentarily forgotten as adrenaline coursed through her veins. "I don't know," she admitted. "But it's the best lead we've got right now. We need to dig deeper into Walsh's background, see if there's anything else that connects him to this case."

She reached for her laptop, fingers flying across the keyboard as she pulled up Walsh's records. "Let's start with his release date. If he's our guy, he would have gotten out recently."

As they delved further into Marcus Walsh's past, Morgan couldn't shake the feeling that they were finally on the right track. But a nagging voice in the back of her mind whispered a warning: if they were right about Walsh, they weren't dealing with some impulsive killer. This was a man who had waited fifteen years for his revenge. A man with patience, determination, and a carefully cultivated rage.

Morgan leaned in closer to the screen, her eyes narrowing as she scanned the details of Marcus Walsh's past. "Engineering," she murmured, her pulse quickening. "Walsh was an engineer before his conviction."

Derik looked up from his own stack of files, raising an eyebrow. "How does that fit in?"

"Think about it," Morgan said, her voice low and intense. "Engineering requires precision. A mind that understands mechanical systems, cause and effect." She paused, the image of the crime scene flashing vividly in her mind. "That basement... it wasn't just a murder. It was a carefully designed death trap, a mechanism of perfectly executed timing and physics."

She could feel the pieces clicking into place, a chilling certainty settling in her gut. Walsh's background in engineering wasn't just a coincidence. It was the missing link they'd been searching for.

Derik nodded slowly, comprehension dawning on his face. "And Walsh would have had the skills to build something like that."

"Exactly," Morgan breathed, pushing back from the desk and running a hand through her hair. The weight of their discovery pressed down on her, a mix of excitement and dread. "We might have just found our prime suspect."

Their eyes met across the table, a silent understanding passing between them. This was the breakthrough they'd been waiting for, but it also meant they were dealing with a killer far more dangerous than they'd initially thought.

Morgan considered their next steps. "We need to track down Walsh's current whereabouts," she said, already reaching for her phone. "And we should look into any properties he might have access to. If he's our guy, he'll need a place to plan and build his... contraptions."

As she dialed, Morgan couldn't shake the image of Walsh, a man who'd spent fifteen years nurturing his resentment, honing his skills, and planning his revenge. A shiver ran down her spine. They were no longer chasing a shadow. They had a name, a face, and a motive.

But would it be enough to catch him before he struck again?

CHAPTER SEVEN

The gravel crunched under the tires as Morgan eased the car to a stop in front of the small church. She squinted against the late afternoon sun, its rays painting long shadows across the humble building and its sparse parking lot. A simple wooden sign caught her eye: "Hope & Redemption Ministry."

Morgan turned to Derik, her brow furrowed. "This can't be right. Are you sure this is the address for Marcus Walsh?"

Derik double-checked his notes and nodded. "Yeah, this is it. Not exactly what I pictured for a guy with his record."

Morgan stepped out of the car. She'd been expecting a rundown apartment or maybe a seedy bar—not this quaint little church on the outskirts of town. The disconnect made her uneasy, heightening her already razor-sharp senses.

"Let's see what we're dealing with," she muttered, more to herself than to Derik.

They approached the entrance, the wooden steps creaking beneath their feet. Morgan hesitated for a moment before pushing open the door, her hand instinctively brushing against her holstered weapon.

The interior was as modest as the exterior—worn pews, faded hymnals, and a small pulpit at the front. And there, arranging flowers on the altar, was a man Morgan almost didn't recognize from the mug shot she'd studied earlier.

"Marcus Walsh?" she called out, her voice echoing in the empty sanctuary.

The man turned, and Morgan felt a jolt of surprise. Gone was the scowling, defiant face she'd seen in his prison photo. This Marcus Walsh had clear eyes, a serene expression, and an air of quiet composure that seemed entirely at odds with his violent past.

"Can I help you?" he asked, his voice soft but steady.

Morgan stepped forward, Derik a half-step behind her. "I'm Special Agent Morgan Cross, this is my partner Special Agent Derik Greene. We'd like to ask you a few questions if you don't mind."

Walsh nodded, setting down the flowers. "Of course. What can I do for you?"

As they began their questioning, Morgan couldn't shake her discomfort. This man—calm, articulate, seemingly at peace—was so far removed from the angry convict she'd expected that she found herself struggling to reconcile the two images.

Is this an act? She wondered. *Or has he really changed this much?*

She pressed on, her tone professional but probing. "Mr. Walsh, can you tell us where you were three nights ago, between the hours of 8 PM and midnight?"

Walsh's brow furrowed slightly, but his demeanor remained tranquil. "I was here at the church, Agent. We were hosting a community dinner and prayer service that evening. Is something wrong?"

Morgan exchanged a quick glance with Derik. This wasn't at all how she'd imagined this confrontation going. She'd come prepared for hostility, for lies, for the need to break down a hardened criminal. Instead, she found herself facing a man who seemed genuinely confused by their presence and entirely willing to cooperate.

Morgan studied Marcus Walsh's face, searching for any hint of deception. His eyes, once hard and filled with anger in his mug shot, now radiated a serene warmth. The transformation was striking, almost unbelievable. She'd seen her fair share of cons and manipulators, but this... this felt different.

"Mr. Walsh," Morgan began, her voice measured, "I understand you've undergone quite a change since your time in prison. Could you tell us more about that?"

Walsh's face softened, a small smile playing at the corners of his mouth. "It's not an easy story to tell, but I'm happy to share it. In prison, I was angry, bitter, lashing out at the world. But then I found faith. It wasn't instantaneous—it was a long, difficult journey. But through it, I found peace and purpose."

As he spoke, Morgan noticed the way his hands remained open and relaxed on the table, a contrast to the clenched fists she often saw in interrogation rooms. His body language screamed openness, vulnerability even.

Is this really the same man who was convicted of manslaughter? Morgan wondered, her skepticism warring with the evidence before her eyes.

Derik leaned forward, his tone curious rather than confrontational. "That's quite a transformation, Mr. Walsh. How has this change manifested in your daily life?"

Walsh's eyes lit up, as if he'd been waiting for this very question. "The most significant change is the vow of nonviolence I've taken. It's not just about not harming others physically—it's a complete shift in how I approach conflict and anger. I've dedicated myself to peace, to finding solutions that don't involve hurting anyone, no matter the circumstances."

Morgan felt a twinge of disappointment. If Walsh was telling the truth—and everything about him suggested he was—then they were back to square one with their investigation. But she couldn't shake the feeling that this encounter, however unproductive for the case, was significant in some way she couldn't yet grasp.

"That's a serious commitment," Morgan said, her tone softening despite herself. "How do you maintain it, especially given your past?"

Walsh's gaze became distant for a moment, as if looking inward. "It's a daily choice, Agent Cross. Every morning, I remind myself of the harm I've caused in the past and recommit to being a force for good in the world. It's not always easy, but it's the path I've chosen."

As Walsh spoke, Morgan found herself believing him. The quiet conviction in his voice, the open vulnerability in his expression—it all pointed to a man who had truly changed. And yet, a small part of her couldn't help but wonder if they were being expertly manipulated.

Morgan leaned forward, her eyes narrowing slightly. Despite Walsh's apparent sincerity, she couldn't afford to take anything at face value. Not with a case this critical.

"I appreciate your openness, Mr. Walsh," she said, her tone professional but probing. "But I need to ask you directly: Where were you on the night of Judge Hawthorne's murder? Can you account for your whereabouts?"

She watched Walsh carefully, looking for any sign of hesitation or discomfort. But his serene expression didn't waver.

Walsh nodded without a moment's pause. "Of course. I understand you need to be thorough." He folded his hands on the table between them. "I've been here at the church for the past week, actually. We're running a community outreach program—providing meals, counseling, and support for those in need."

Morgan raised an eyebrow. "That's quite a commitment. Can anyone corroborate your presence here?"

"Absolutely," Walsh replied, his voice steady. "We have volunteers working around the clock, and I've been here every day and night.

Pastor Jim, our kitchen staff, the other counselors—they can all confirm I haven't left the premises."

As Walsh spoke, Morgan found herself caught between skepticism and a growing belief in his words. His alibi seemed solid, almost too convenient. And yet, there was an authenticity to his demeanor that was hard to fake.

Could he really have changed this much? Morgan wondered. *Or is this all an elaborate act?*

She decided to push a little harder. "That's quite a transformation from your past, Mr. Walsh. Some might find it hard to believe."

Walsh's eyes softened, a hint of sadness creeping into his expression. "I understand the doubt. I've doubted myself many times on this journey. But my faith, and the support of this community, have given me strength I never knew I had."

Morgan felt a conflicting mix of emotions. Part of her wanted to believe in redemption, in the possibility of real change. But the detective in her couldn't ignore the stakes of their investigation.

"We'll need to verify your alibi, of course," she said, her tone matter-of-fact.

Walsh nodded, his expression open. "Of course. I'll provide you with all the contact information you need. I have nothing to hide."

As Morgan jotted down the details, she couldn't shake the feeling that their lead had just evaporated. If Walsh's story checked out—and her instincts were telling her it would—they were back to square one.

Morgan's eyes met Derik's, a silent understanding passing between them. The tension in her shoulders eased slightly as she recognized the truth reflected in her partner's gaze. Marcus Walsh wasn't their killer.

She cleared her throat, tucking away her notebook. "Thank you for your time, Mr. Walsh. We'll be in touch if we need anything further."

Walsh nodded, his demeanor still serene. "I hope you find who you're looking for, Agents. May God guide your path."

Morgan zipped up her leather jacket, the late afternoon chill nipping at her skin as she and Derik made their way across the church's gravel parking lot. The setting sun cast long shadows, painting the modest building in shades of amber and gold. She couldn't shake the feeling of disappointment that clung to her like a second skin. Another dead end.

As they approached their car, a voice called out behind them. "Agents, wait."

Morgan turned to see Marcus Walsh jogging towards them, his face etched with an expression of deep contemplation. She tensed instinctively, her hand hovering near her holster, but Walsh's body language remained open and non-threatening.

"Is everything alright, Mr. Walsh?" she asked, studying his face carefully.

Walsh nodded, his eyes meeting hers with an intensity that made Morgan's skin prickle. "I've been thinking about your case, about Judge Hawthorne," he said, his voice low and thoughtful. "There's something I think you should consider."

Morgan exchanged a quick glance with Derik before turning her full attention back to Walsh. "We're listening," she said, curiosity piqued despite her wariness.

Walsh took a deep breath, as if steeling himself. "The person who set up that trap... they didn't actually kill Judge Hawthorne. The trap did."

The words hung in the air between them, heavy with implication. Morgan felt her breath catch in her throat, her mind racing to process this new perspective.

"What do you mean?" she asked, her voice barely above a whisper.

Walsh's eyes took on a faraway look, as if he was seeing something beyond their immediate surroundings. "In my time inside, I've seen all kinds of justifications for violence. But this... this is different. The killer didn't pull the trigger themselves. They created a situation, a choice."

Morgan's heart pounded in her chest as she absorbed Walsh's words. The pieces of the puzzle were shifting, realigning in her mind to form a new, disturbing picture.

"You're saying the killer sees themselves as separate from the act," she said slowly, the implications making her stomach churn.

Walsh nodded solemnly. "It's a dangerous mindset. One that allows them to distance themselves from the consequences of their actions."

As Morgan stared at Walsh, she couldn't help but wonder what demons he had faced, what transformations he had undergone to reach this level of insight. And more pressingly, how this new perspective would reshape their investigation.

"Thank you, Mr. Walsh," she said finally, her voice thick with the weight of this revelation. "You've given us a lot to think about."

As they drove away from the church, Morgan's mind whirled with possibilities. The killer they were hunting wasn't just a murderer - they were something far more complex and potentially more dangerous.

Someone who believed they could play judge, jury, and executioner without getting their hands dirty.

The sun dipped below the horizon, casting the world in twilight. And in the gathering darkness, Morgan felt the case taking on a new, more sinister shape.

Morgan's fingers tapped restlessly on the steering wheel as she navigated the darkening streets. The weight of Walsh's words hung heavy in the air between her and Derik.

"It's a twisted logic," she murmured, breaking the tense silence. "The killer's created a moral loophole for themselves."

Derik shifted in his seat, his brow furrowed. "You think Walsh is onto something?"

Morgan nodded, her eyes fixed on the road ahead. "It fits. The elaborate setup, the chance for escape... it's like they're trying to absolve themselves of responsibility."

She could feel the pieces clicking into place, a grim picture forming in her mind. The killer wasn't just seeking revenge; they were crafting a narrative, one where they weren't directly responsible for the death.

"It's like they're saying, 'I didn't kill him, the trap did,'" Morgan continued, her voice tight with frustration. "As if that makes it any less murder."

Derik leaned back, his expression thoughtful. "It's a hell of a psychological trick. Gives them a way to sleep at night, I guess."

Morgan's grip tightened on the wheel. "But why go to all this trouble? Why not just..." She trailed off, unable to finish the thought.

"Because it's not about efficiency," Derik said softly. "It's about proving a point."

Morgan felt a chill run down her spine. The killer wasn't just taking lives; they were crafting elaborate scenarios, giving their victims a slim chance at survival. It was a game, a terrible, deadly game.

"We're not just looking for a murderer," she said, her voice barely above a whisper. "We're looking for someone who sees themselves as above the law, above morality. Someone who thinks they have the right to put people on trial."

Derik shifted in his seat, his brow furrowed. "You think they're trying to cleanse their conscience? By giving the victims a chance, however slim?"

Morgan shook her head, her eyes narrowing. "It's more than that. This killer... they're playing God. Setting up these elaborate traps, these twisted courtrooms – it's all about control. About passing judgment."

She turned to face her partner, her expression grim. "They're not just avoiding blood on their hands. They're creating a whole system, a perverse form of justice where they get to decide who lives and who dies."

Derik let out a low whistle. "That's one hell of an ego trip."

"And one hell of a dangerous mentality," Morgan added, her voice tight. "We're not just chasing a murderer anymore. We're up against someone who truly believes they're above the law, above morality itself."

As they stepped out of the car, the weight of this realization settled heavily on Morgan's shoulders. The cool evening air did little to calm the storm of thoughts in her mind.

"We need to re-examine everything," she said, striding towards the precinct doors. "Every detail of the crime scene, every piece of evidence. Our killer isn't just playing a game – they're creating a system. And that makes them infinitely more dangerous than we initially thought."

Derik nodded, falling into step beside her. "Where do we even start with something like this?"

Morgan paused at the entrance, her hand on the door. "We start by thinking like they do. We need to understand their twisted logic, their warped sense of justice. Only then can we hope to catch them before they strike again."

As they entered the bustling precinct, Morgan couldn't shake the feeling that they were running out of time. Somewhere out there, their killer was likely already planning their next "trial" – and she was determined to stop them before another innocent life was lost to their perverted notion of justice.

CHAPTER EIGHT

The glass-and-steel monoliths of downtown cast long shadows across the parking garage as Michelle Knox stepped out of her office building. The last vestiges of sunlight glinted off skyscraper windows, bathing the city in an orange glow that was rapidly fading to dusk. Her heels clicked a staccato rhythm on the pavement as she made her way toward her car, the sound echoing in the near-empty garage.

Michelle rolled her neck, trying to ease the tension that had built up over hours hunched over spreadsheets and financial reports. Numbers still danced behind her eyelids when she blinked—profit margins, quarterly projections, investment portfolios. She'd been staring at screens for so long, the real world seemed slightly out of focus.

"Another day, another dollar," she muttered to herself, fishing in her purse for her car keys. "Or a few million dollars, in this case."

As an investment analyst for one of the city's top firms, Michelle was used to high-stakes decisions and long hours. But today had been particularly grueling. Back-to-back meetings with anxious clients, followed by an emergency strategy session when the market took an unexpected dip. She'd barely had time to grab a wilted salad from the break room fridge for lunch.

Now, all she wanted was to get home, kick off these pinching heels, and pour herself a generous glass of cabernet. Maybe order some takeout and binge a few episodes of that new crime drama everyone was talking about. Anything to quiet the ceaseless whirring of her mind.

As she approached her sleek black sedan, Michelle's thoughts drifted to the bottle of wine chilling in her fridge. A small indulgence, but one she felt she'd more than earned today.

"You deserve it, Knox," she told herself, allowing a small smile. "Hell, maybe even splurge on the good stuff tonight. Life's too short for cheap wine."

The parking garage was eerily quiet, most of her coworkers having left hours ago. Michelle's footsteps echoed off the concrete pillars, and she found herself picking up her pace slightly. She'd never admit to being nervous—she prided herself on her cool head under pressure—

but there was something unsettling about being alone in such a vast, empty space as night fell.

She clicked the key fob, and her car's lights flashed in greeting. The familiar sight eased some of the tension in her shoulders. Just a few more steps, and she'd be on her way home.

"Early night tonight," she mused, reaching for the door handle. "Maybe I can actually catch up on some sleep for once. Novel concept."

As she slid into the driver's seat, Michelle let out a long exhale, feeling the day's stress begin to ebb away. She tossed her purse onto the passenger seat and took a moment to close her eyes, savoring the quiet. Tomorrow would bring new challenges, new fires to put out. But for now, she could leave it all behind and focus on unwinding.

"Alright, Knox," she said, starting the engine. "Home, wine, relaxation. In that order."

With a final glance at the darkening sky visible through the garage's concrete levels, Michelle put the car in drive and headed for the exit, leaving the long day—and the looming shadows—behind her.

Michelle's hand froze on the door handle, her breath catching in her throat. A figure materialized from the shadows, leaning against her sleek black sedan. Her analytical mind, honed by years of dissecting market trends, instantly cataloged details: male, medium build, dark clothing blending into the twilight gloom of the parking garage.

"Excuse me," she called out, her voice echoing unnaturally in the cavernous space. "That's my car you're leaning on."

The man didn't react. He remained motionless, head tilted downward as if studying the cracked concrete beneath his feet. Michelle's eyes narrowed, her body tensing as she assessed the situation.

This isn't right, she thought, her mind racing. *Security should have cleared the garage by now. Why isn't he responding?*

"Sir?" she tried again, taking a cautious step closer. "I need to get to my car. Are you alright?"

Still no response. The unnatural stillness sent a chill down Michelle's spine. She'd dealt with aggressive personalities in boardrooms, navigated high-stakes negotiations, but this... this was different. The man's presence felt deliberate, calculated.

He's waiting for something, she realized, her analytical instincts kicking into overdrive. *Or someone.*

Michelle's gaze darted around the garage, searching for any sign of security or other late-night workers. The emptiness suddenly felt oppressive.

"Look," she said, injecting steel into her voice, "I don't know what you're doing here, but I'm leaving now. Step away from my car."

The man's head lifted slightly, but in the dim light, Michelle couldn't make out his features. His posture remained slouched, almost unnaturally so. Something about the way he held himself set off alarm bells in her mind.

This isn't some drunk who wandered in, she thought. *He's too... controlled. Too deliberate.*

Michelle's mind raced through scenarios, weighing options. Should she turn and run? Try to bluff her way past him? Call for help? The analytical part of her brain that had served her so well in her career now felt like both a blessing and a curse, presenting her with an overwhelming array of potential outcomes.

Michelle's fingers tightened around the pepper spray in her purse, the cool metal grounding her. Her heart hammered against her ribs, but years of high-pressure meetings had taught her to keep her voice steady.

"Hey!" she called out, infusing her tone with the same authority she used to command boardrooms. "Back off."

The command hung in the air, echoing slightly in the cavernous garage. For a moment, Michelle thought the man hadn't heard her. Then, slowly, almost mechanically, he stirred.

His head lifted, and Michelle's breath caught in her throat. Even in the dim lighting, she could see his eyes – unfocused, glassy, as if looking through her rather than at her. A chill ran down her spine.

The man swayed slightly, barely keeping his balance. His movements were sluggish, almost puppet-like. Michelle's grip on the pepper spray tightened.

"I said back off," she repeated, taking a small step to the side. "I don't want any trouble."

The man's mouth opened, but no words came out. Instead, a low, guttural sound emerged – not quite a groan, not quite speech. Michelle's skin crawled.

"Look," Michelle said, trying to keep her voice calm despite the growing panic in her chest, "I'm going to call security if you don't move away from my car right now."

She reached for her phone with her free hand, never taking her eyes off the swaying figure. The man's head tilted, as if processing her words through a fog. His unfocused gaze drifted past her, towards the garage entrance.

Michelle's instincts screamed at her to run, but she held her ground. *If I turn my back, I'm vulnerable,* she reasoned. *I need to stay in control of this situation.*

"Last chance," she warned, her finger hovering over the emergency call button. "Move, or I'm calling for help."

The man finally seemed to register her words. With agonizing slowness, he shuffled away from her car, his feet dragging as if weighed down by invisible chains. Michelle exhaled, a shaky breath she hadn't realized she'd been holding.

Maybe he really is just drunk, she thought, watching him stumble towards a concrete pillar. *God, I'm getting paranoid.*

Still, the tension in her chest refused to uncoil completely. Michelle kept her eyes on the retreating figure, unwilling to let her guard down just yet. The pepper spray remained clutched in her sweaty palm, a comforting weight.

"Okay," she muttered to herself, fumbling for her keys. "Let's get out of here."

Her analytical mind, however, wouldn't let go of the encounter so easily. As she turned back to her car, Michelle's thoughts raced. *His movements were too uncoordinated for just alcohol. Could it be some kind of medical condition? Or--*

The sudden pressure against her face cut off all rational thought. A large hand clamped over her nose and mouth, an iron grip she couldn't shake. Michelle's world narrowed to the overpowering stench of chemicals flooding her senses – sharp, medicinal, with an underlying sweetness that made her stomach lurch.

Panic exploded through her body. Michelle's free hand clawed at her attacker, but her nails met only the slick surface of what felt like rubber gloves. She tried to scream, but the sound was muffled against the cloth pressed to her face.

No, no, no! Her mind raced, searching for options for an escape. The pepper spray – still in her hand, if she could just aim it behind her--

But her limbs felt increasingly heavy, uncooperative. The garage lights blurred, stretching into strange halos. Michelle's last coherent thought before consciousness began to slip away was a realization that chilled her to her core:

Michelle's body thrashed wildly, every fiber of her being screaming to fight. But the more she struggled, the tighter the cloth pressed against her face, suffocating her. Her lungs burned, desperate for clean air. The world around her began to spin, colors blurring into a nauseating kaleidoscope.

"Stop... fighting," a gruff voice hissed in her ear. "It'll be over soon."

No! Michelle's mind rebelled, even as her body began to betray her. Her legs, once so steady in her power walks to meetings, now felt like jelly. She tried to kick backward, to stomp on her attacker's foot, but her movements were uncoordinated, weak.

"Why..." she managed to gasp out, the word muffled against the chemical-soaked cloth. "Who..."

The strength was rapidly draining from her body. Michelle's arms, toned from countless hours at the gym, felt alien to her now – heavy, sluggish, as if they belonged to someone else. She tried to raise them, to claw at her attacker's face, but they barely twitched.

Her knees buckled, no longer able to support her weight. As Michelle felt herself falling, she made one last, desperate attempt to fight. Her fingers, still clutching her car keys, loosened their grip.

The metallic clatter of keys hitting concrete echoed in her fading consciousness. It was such a small sound, yet to Michelle, it felt like the tolling of a bell – marking the moment her world changed forever.

As darkness engulfed her, Michelle's last coherent thought was a mixture of disbelief and anger: *How dare they. How dare they think they can take me.*

Then, there was nothing but silence and the cold embrace of oblivion.

CHAPTER NINE

Morgan leaned back in her chair, her eyes burning from hours of staring at case files. The briefing room felt like a tomb, silent except for the low hum of computer monitors.

She rubbed her temples, willing away the headache that threatened to consume her. The wall of evidence before her was a twisted tapestry of death and deceit. Somewhere in this web of information was the key to unlocking the truth behind Judge Hawthorne's murder.

Morgan's gaze fell to the file open on the desk before her. Sarah Reeves. Former law clerk to the murdered judge. Sarah had died by suicide a year ago, according to the file, which didn't seem relevant, at first glance, but then again, Morgan didn't have much else to go off. She found herself curious to know more.

"What's your story, Sarah?" Morgan murmured, her fingers tracing the edge of the file. "What secrets did you take to the grave?"

She flipped through the pages, searching for anything that might connect Reeves to Hawthorne's murder. But the more she read, the more questions arose. Reeves had been found in her bathtub, wrists slit, a half-empty bottle of pills on the counter. A note, tearstained and crumpled, lay nearby.

"I can't go on like this," Morgan read aloud, her voice barely above a whisper. "The pain is too much. I'm sorry."

Something nagged at her. A gut feeling she couldn't shake.

"Why now?" she asked the empty room. "Why, after all this time, am I looking at your case, Sarah?"

Morgan's gaze drifted to Judge Hawthorne's photo. His stern face stared back at her, offering no answers. Maybe it was just a coincidence that a year before his own brutal murder, his law clerk died by suicide, someone very close to him. But something about it nagged at her.

The door creaked open behind her, and Morgan spun around, instinctively reaching for her weapon. She relaxed when she saw Derik's familiar face, his green eyes tired but alert as he balanced two steaming cups of coffee.

"Thought you could use a pick-me-up," he said, setting one of the cups in front of her.

Morgan nodded gratefully, wrapping her hands around the warm mug. "Thanks, Derik. I was just thinking—"

"That there's more to this case than meets the eye?" Derik finished, a wry smile playing on his lips. "I could hear the gears turning from down the hall."

She took a sip of coffee, savoring the bitter taste. "I can't shake the feeling that we're missing something crucial. I was just looking into this—Sarah Reeves, Hawthorne's law clerk, died by suicide about a year ago."

Derik leaned against the desk, his brow furrowed. "You think there's a connection between the two deaths?"

"I think it's worth exploring," Morgan replied, her voice firm. "We need to dig deeper into Hawthorne's rulings, see if there's any case that stands out. Someone who might have had a grudge against both Hawthorne and Reeves. I don't know, maybe Reeves's death wasn't a suicide at all."

She turned back to the board, her eyes scanning the information for the hundredth time. The weight of the case pressed down on her, mingling with the ever-present tension of her own unresolved past.

"Whoever did this," Morgan said softly, "they went to a lot of trouble to make a point. The question is, what were they trying to say? And to whom?"

Derik's eyes softened as he watched Morgan, her intense focus etched into every line of her face. He placed a gentle hand on her shoulder.

"Morgan, you need to take a break," he said, his voice laced with concern. "Step away for a few hours, maybe get some sleep. You've been at this forever."

Morgan scoffed, but didn't shrug off his hand. "I'm fine, Derik. We're close to something, I can feel it."

"You always say that," he replied, a hint of exasperation creeping into his tone. "But you're not a machine. You need rest to function properly."

She turned to face him, her dark eyes burning with a mix of determination and something deeper, more vulnerable. "I can't stop now. Not when we're this close."

Derik sighed, recognizing the stubbornness in her stance. "It's not just about Hawthorne's murder, is it?" he asked softly.

Morgan's jaw clenched, her fingers tightening around the coffee mug. She wanted to deny it, to focus solely on the case at hand, but Derik knew her too well.

"No," she admitted, her voice barely above a whisper. "It's about Cordell."

The name hung in the air between them, heavy with unspoken implications. Morgan's mind raced with images of the man who had orchestrated her downfall, who had stolen a decade of her life.

"He's still out there," she continued, her voice gaining strength. "Watching, waiting. Even as I try to focus on the case, I know he's biding his time, waiting to take me—us—down."

Derik nodded, understanding dawning in his eyes. "And your father?"

Morgan's breath caught in her throat. John Christopher. The man she had mourned, only to discover he was alive. The revelation had shaken her to her core, reopening old wounds and creating new ones.

"He's safe, I think," she said, the words tasting bitter on her tongue. "Alive, but might as well be a ghost. Until we deal with Cordell, I can't... I can't even think about what comes next with him."

She turned back to the evidence board, her eyes tracing the web of connections they'd mapped out. "So I keep working. Keep focusing on the case. Because as long as I'm chasing this killer, I don't have to face the one who's been haunting me for years."

Derik's hand squeezed her shoulder gently, a silent gesture of support and understanding. Morgan leaned into his touch, allowing herself a moment of vulnerability in the dim glow of the briefing room.

Morgan's fingers traced the edge of Sarah Reeves' file, her mind churning with possibilities. The weight of her father's absence pressed heavily on her chest, but she pushed it aside, focusing on the task at hand.

"What if we're looking at this all wrong?" she mused, half to herself and half to Derik. "What if Reeves' death wasn't a suicide at all?"

Derik leaned in, his brow furrowed. "You think it's connected to Hawthorne's murder?"

Morgan nodded, her eyes never leaving the crime scene photos. "It's too neat. Too convenient. A law clerk with supposed mental health issues takes her own life, and then a year later, the judge she worked for ends up dead in an elaborate death trap?"

She stood, pacing the length of the evidence board. Her ankle, still healing from her encounter in the woods, twinged with each step, a constant reminder of the secrets lurking just beneath the surface of her life.

"We need to dig deeper into Reeves' background," Morgan said, her voice tight with determination. "Family, friends, coworkers. Someone must have noticed something off about her behavior leading up to her death."

Derik watched her, concern etched on his face. "Morgan, are you sure this isn't about-"

"It's about finding the truth," she cut him off, perhaps too sharply. She took a breath, steadying herself. "I know what you're thinking, but this isn't about Cordell. This is about justice for Hawthorne and potentially for Reeves too."

But even as the words left her mouth, Morgan couldn't shake the feeling that everything - every case, every victim - was somehow connected to the shadowy figure of Richard Cordell. His presence loomed over her life like a storm cloud, dark and threatening.

She turned back to Derik, her eyes blazing with a mix of determination and barely concealed fear. "We follow this lead. We find out what really happened. And maybe, just maybe, it'll lead us one step closer to understanding what happened to Hawthorne."

CHAPTER TEN

Michelle's eyelids fluttered open, her vision blurry and unfocused. For a brief, blissful moment, she thought she was in a hospital. The familiar antiseptic scent tickled her nostrils, mingling with the crisp aroma of freshly laundered linens. Cool sheets pressed against her skin, a stark contrast to the feverish heat radiating from her body. The dull beep of machines filled the air, a rhythmic pulse that should have been comforting but instead sent an inexplicable chill down her spine.

A dim, sterile light glowed from overhead, casting long shadows across the room. Michelle blinked rapidly, trying to bring her surroundings into focus. The ceiling tiles above her swam in and out of view, their stark whiteness almost painful to her sensitive eyes.

"Hello?" she called out, her voice hoarse and unfamiliar to her own ears. "Is anyone there?"

Silence answered her, broken only by the steady beep-beep-beep of the monitors. Michelle's heart rate quickened, each beat echoing the machine's relentless rhythm. Something was wrong. Very wrong.

She tried to sit up, but her body felt leaden, unresponsive. Panic bubbled up in her chest, threatening to overwhelm her. This wasn't right. Where was the nurse? The doctor? Anyone?

"Help," she croaked, her throat dry and raw. "I need help!"

Still no response. Michelle's mind raced, desperately trying to piece together how she'd ended up here. The last thing she remembered was leaving the office late, her briefcase heavy with reports for tomorrow's big presentation. Had there been an accident? A sudden illness?

She forced herself to take a deep breath, drawing on the calm rationality that had served her so well in the cutthroat world of investment banking. "Think, Michelle," she muttered to herself. "Assess the situation. Find a solution."

But as she lay there, trying to make sense of her surroundings, a creeping sense of dread settled over her. The room was too quiet, too still. Even in the middle of the night, a real hospital would have some signs of life - distant footsteps, murmured conversations, the squeak of a cart being wheeled down a hallway.

This place was like a tomb.

Something was very, very wrong. And as Michelle lay there, surrounded by the eerie beeping of machines and bathed in that sickly, sterile light, she couldn't shake the feeling that her ordeal was only just beginning.

Michelle's head throbbed as she tried to process her surroundings. The nausea intensified, churning her stomach like a violent sea. She gritted her teeth, fighting the urge to retch.

"Got to... get up," she mumbled, her words slurring slightly. With monumental effort, Michelle pushed herself into a sitting position. The sudden movement sent the room spinning, and she swayed dangerously, gripping the edge of the bed to steady herself.

"What... what's happening to me?" she gasped, her breath coming in short, panicked bursts. The dizziness was overwhelming, worse than any hangover she'd experienced after late nights closing deals. This felt... wrong. Unnatural.

As her vision slowly stabilized, Michelle's gaze fell on the medical equipment surrounding her bed. Something about it nagged at her foggy mind. She squinted, trying to focus.

"Wait a minute," she muttered, leaning closer to examine the heart monitor. The numbers on the display didn't fluctuate, remaining perfectly static despite her elevated heart rate. "That's not right."

Her eyes darted to the IV stand, then the ventilator. Each piece looked convincing at first glance, but upon closer inspection, they were clearly not functional medical devices.

"Props," Michelle whispered, a chill running down her spine. "They're all props. But why? What kind of sick game is this?"

Michelle's heart raced as she yanked at the wires and tubes attached to her body. They came away easily, revealing adhesive pads instead of proper medical connections. Her hands shook as she tossed them aside, the plastic clattering against the tiled floor.

Gritting her teeth against the dizziness, Michelle pushed herself upright. Her muscles felt like lead, responding sluggishly to her commands. Still, she managed to swing her legs over the side of the bed, surprised to find she wasn't restrained.

"Hello?" she called out, her voice echoing in the sterile room. "Is anyone there? What's going on?"

Silence answered her. Michelle's eyes darted around the room, searching for cameras for any sign of who might be watching her. The walls were bare, save for a single mirror that she strongly suspected was two-way glass.

She was about to attempt standing when a voice suddenly filled the room. It was low and mechanical, distorted beyond recognition, sending chills down her spine.

"Welcome to your worst nightmare, Michelle Knox," the voice intoned, emotionless yet somehow menacing.

Michelle's breath caught in her throat. "Who are you? What do you want from me?"

The voice continued, ignoring her questions. "Your skills have served you well in the cutthroat world of finance. But how will they fare when your life is on the line?" The mechanical voice cut through her racing thoughts like a knife. "You have been poisoned."

Michelle froze, her body suddenly rigid with fear. Her breath came in short, rapid gasps, her pulse hammering against her ribs so violently she could feel it in her throat.

"In three minutes, your heart will stop," the voice continued, its robotic tone a stark contrast to the devastating message it delivered. "The antidote is hidden somewhere in the room."

Michelle's mind reeled, struggling to process the information. Poison? Antidote? This couldn't be real. But the nausea churning in her stomach, the dizziness clouding her thoughts – they felt all too genuine.

"This is absurd," she hissed through clenched teeth, even as her eyes began frantically scanning the room. "You can't just – this has to be illegal. I'll sue you for everything you're worth!"

Her bravado crumbled as another wave of nausea hit her, more intense than before. Michelle's stomach clenched in terror, her fingers trembling as she gripped the edge of the bed, trying to steady herself. A cold sweat broke out along her skin, her designer blouse now clinging uncomfortably to her back.

"Oh God," she whispered, the reality of her situation sinking in. Her heart was racing too fast, too erratically. What if it was true? What if she really only had minutes left to live?

Panic overwhelmed her carefully cultivated composure. Michelle's throat constricted, and a raw, desperate scream tore from her lips. "HELP! Somebody help me, please!"

Her voice bounced off the cold, sterile walls, swallowed by the oppressive silence of the room.

But no matter how long Michelle called out, no response came.

CHAPTER ELEVEN

The soft glow of the desk lamp cast long shadows across Morgan's living room, illuminating the stacks of case files spread across her coffee table like miniature skyscrapers of manila and white. Morgan's eyes burned, her vision blurring as she stared at the documents before her. The weight of exhaustion pressed against her like a physical force, but she stubbornly refused to give in to sleep.

"Just a little longer," she muttered to herself, rubbing her temples. "There has to be something here I'm missing."

Morgan shifted, uncrossing and recrossing her legs on the hardwood floor. Beside her, Skunk's rhythmic breathing was the only steady sound in the otherwise silent house. The big dog's presence was comforting, a warm, solid weight against her thigh.

She glanced across the room to where Derik lay sprawled on her couch, one arm draped over his face. His chest rose and fell in the slow cadence of deep sleep. A pang of guilt twisted in Morgan's gut. She should have sent him home hours ago, but a selfish part of her had wanted him to stay.

"Some partner I am," she whispered, careful not to wake him. "Making you pull an all-nighter on a case that's going nowhere."

Morgan's gaze drifted back to the files, her mind churning. She reached for her coffee mug, grimacing at the cold dregs within. The bitter taste did little to clear the fog from her mind. Morgan set the mug down with a soft clink, her fingers trailing over the handle.

"Dad," she breathed, the word barely audible. "What would you do?"

The memory of John Christopher's face flashed in her mind—alive, after all these years. The revelation still felt surreal, like a dream she might wake from at any moment. She closed her eyes, picturing the determination in his gaze as he'd explained everything to her in that hidden shack.

"Focus on what you know," she could almost hear him say. "Build from there."

Morgan's eyes snapped open. She reached for a notepad, scribbling furiously as her thoughts coalesced.

A soft whine from Skunk pulled her from her reverie. The dog's tail thumped gently against the floor as he lifted his head, dark eyes fixed on her with concern.

Morgan managed a tired smile, reaching out to scratch behind his ears. "I'm okay, boy," she assured him. "Just trying to put the pieces together."

Skunk huffed, unconvinced, and rested his chin on her knee. Morgan's smile softened as she stroked his fur, grateful for the companionship.

"What do you think, Skunk?" she asked quietly. "Any insights into our mystery killer?"

The dog's only response was to snuffle and press closer against her side. Morgan chuckled softly, her gaze drifting back to the sleeping form of her partner.

"At least one of us is getting some rest," she mused.

With a sigh, Morgan turned back to her notes. Sleep could wait. She had a killer to catch.

Morgan's eyes burned as she sifted through the sea of documents before her. Hawthorne's cases blurred into an indistinguishable mass of legal jargon and dates. She blinked hard, trying to focus on the details that mattered. Sentences handed down, lives irrevocably altered by the stroke of Hawthorne's pen. There had to be something here, some thread connecting the judge's death to this elaborate staging.

"Dammit," she muttered, rubbing her temples. "What am I missing?"

Skunk's ears perked up at the sound of her voice, but he remained nestled against her side, a warm, comforting presence. Across the room, Derik stirred slightly in his sleep, mumbling something incoherent before settling back into silence.

Morgan's gaze fell on a familiar name: Sarah Reeves. The young law clerk's file lay open atop a stack of papers, her smiling face staring up from an old employee ID photo. Morgan reached for it, her fingers tracing the edge of the photograph.

"Why you?" she whispered. "What's your connection to all this?"

She scanned the report again, searching for any detail she might have overlooked. Depression. Deteriorating mental state. Suicide. The words were clinical, detached, reducing a vibrant young woman to a tragic statistic.

Morgan closed her eyes, trying to picture Sarah as she must have been – ambitious, driven, working long hours under Hawthorne's exacting standards. What had pushed her over the edge? Was it really just the pressure of the job, or was there something more?

"There has to be more to your story, Sarah," Morgan murmured. "What aren't these reports telling me?"

She flipped through the pages, looking for anything out of place. Witness statements, medical records, all painting a picture of a woman spiraling into despair. But something nagged at Morgan, a persistent feeling that she was missing a crucial piece of the puzzle.

"If you were connected to Hawthorne's death," she reasoned aloud, "why wait a year?"

Morgan's fingers traced the edge of Sarah Reeves' file, her mind churning with possibilities. She wanted—needed—there to be a connection between Sarah's death and Hawthorne's murder. But the more she searched, the more elusive that link became.

She closed her eyes, trying to visualize the timeline. Sarah's suicide, a year ago. Hawthorne's murder, just a day ago.

Morgan exhaled heavily, rubbing her temples. The headache that had been threatening all evening was now pounding behind her eyes. "Focus," she commanded herself. "There has to be something I'm missing."

She reached for her coffee mug, grimacing as she swallowed the cold dregs. As she set it down, her gaze fell on a small detail in Sarah's file—a notation about a therapist Sarah had been seeing in the months before her death.

"Dr. Elaine Foster," Morgan read aloud. "Maybe you can shed some light on—"

The shrill ring of her phone cut through the silence like a knife, jolting Skunk from his peaceful slumber. The dog's head snapped up, his ears perked and alert as Morgan snatched her phone from the coffee table. Her eyes widened as she saw the caller ID: Mueller.

A chill ran down her spine. "If he's calling this late, it can't be good," she muttered, her thumb hovering over the answer button for a split second before she swiped to accept the call.

"Mueller, what's going on?" Morgan asked, her voice tight with tension.

There was a pause on the other end, filled only by the sound of Mueller's heavy breathing. When he finally spoke, his voice was weary, laden with the weight of bad news. "Morgan, we've got another one. Another crime scene."

The words hit her like a physical blow. Morgan's free hand clenched into a fist, her nails digging into her palm. She'd known, deep down, that the killer would strike again, but she'd never expected it to be so soon. The realization made her stomach churn.

"Where?" she managed to ask, already pushing herself to her feet. Skunk whined softly, sensing her distress.

What would they find this time? Another staged scenario? Another victim who'd been given a chance to escape but hadn't made it? The possibilities made her head spin.

"I'm on my way," she said, ending the call. For a moment, she stood still, trying to gather her thoughts. The fatigue that had been weighing on her moments ago was gone, replaced by a surge of adrenaline and a gnawing sense of dread.

"Damn it," she whispered, running a hand through her hair. "We're always one step behind." The frustration in her voice was palpable, echoing in the quiet room. She glanced at the scattered case files, at Sarah Reeves' photo staring up at her. "What are we missing?"

With a deep breath, Morgan steeled herself for what was to come. Another crime scene. Another victim. Another piece of the puzzle that she had to fit together before the killer struck again. The weight of responsibility settled heavily on her shoulders as she moved to wake Derik, knowing that the long night ahead would only be the beginning.

"Derik, wake up," she urged, her voice tight with urgency.

He groaned, his face scrunching up in protest as he slowly stirred. "Wha...? Morgan?" he mumbled, blinking groggily.

But the moment his eyes focused on her face—the taut lines of worry etched around her mouth, the barely contained panic in her eyes—Derik bolted upright, instantly alert. "What's happened?" he asked, already reaching for his shoes.

"Another body," Morgan said, her words clipped. "We need to go. Now."

Derik nodded, no further explanation needed. As he laced up his shoes, Morgan grabbed her jacket, her mind racing. "I knew he'd strike again," she muttered, more to herself than to Derik. "But this soon? What's his game?"

"We'll figure it out," Derik assured her, his voice steady despite the gravity of the situation. It was one of the things Morgan appreciated most about him—his ability to remain calm under pressure.

As they hurried out the door, Morgan paused, looking back at Skunk. The dog whined softly, sensing her distress. "Stay, boy," she commanded gently. "We'll be back soon."

The drive to the crime scene was tense, the roads eerily empty in the pre-dawn hours. Morgan's knuckles were white on the steering wheel, her jaw clenched as she navigated the familiar streets of Dallas.

"What do we know so far?" Derik asked, breaking the heavy silence.

Morgan shook her head. "Not much. Mueller didn't have many details. Just an address and... and confirmation that it's connected to our case."

As they approached their destination, the flashing lights of police cruisers cut through the darkness, a beacon guiding them to the latest horror. Morgan felt her stomach tighten as she pulled up to the curb.

"An abandoned rental space," she murmured, taking in the dilapidated building before them. "Clear across town from the first scene."

Derik's brow furrowed. "He's moving around. Trying to throw us off?"

"Maybe," Morgan replied, unbuckling her seatbelt. "Or maybe location is part of his message." She paused, her hand on the door handle. "You ready for this?"

Derik met her gaze, his eyes reflecting the determination she felt. "As ready as we can be," he said grimly.

Together, they stepped out into the chilly morning air, the weight of what awaited them inside hanging heavy between them. As they approached the crime scene, Morgan steeled herself, knowing that whatever they found beyond that yellow tape would only deepen the mystery—and the urgency—of their investigation.

***

Morgan ducked under the yellow crime scene tape, her nostrils immediately assaulted by the acrid scent of stale air and faint disinfectant. The dimly lit space before her was a sharp contrast to the pre-dawn darkness outside. As her eyes adjusted, she felt Derik's presence close behind her, his breath catching audibly as he took in the scene.

"Jesus," he muttered.

Morgan's stomach twisted violently as she absorbed the full scope of what lay before them. The room had been meticulously staged, but not as a courtroom this time. This was a mockery of a hospital, eerie in its uncanny falseness.

"It's like a twisted dollhouse," Morgan breathed, her voice barely above a whisper. She took a tentative step forward, her eyes roving over the plastic medical equipment, a fake heart monitor with a flat, unmoving line, and a cheap metal bed positioned dead center in the room. IV bags filled with colored liquid hung nearby, a grotesque parody of life-saving medication.

Derik moved to stand beside her, his face pale in the harsh overhead light. "He's escalating. This is... more elaborate than before."

Morgan nodded, her mind racing. "But why a hospital? What's the connection?"

She approached the bed, careful not to disturb anything. The stark walls and sterile shadows made her skin crawl. This level of detail, of premeditation, spoke of a mind both brilliant and deeply disturbed.

Morgan's eyes locked onto the limp form crumpled near the exit. The victim's skin was unnaturally pale, almost translucent in the harsh artificial light. No visible blood, yet death was unmistakable in the unnatural stillness of the body.

Officer Ramirez approached, his face grim. "Agent Cross, we've identified the victim as Michelle Knox, thirty-four years old."

Morgan nodded, her throat tight. "What else can you tell me?"

Ramirez flipped open his notepad. "Knox was an investment banker. No criminal record, lived alone. Neighbors described her as quiet, kept to herself."

As Morgan surveyed the scene, a chill ran down her spine. The elaborately staged hospital room, the body positioned near freedom - it was hauntingly familiar.

"It's another performance," she murmured, more to herself than to Ramirez.

Derik stepped closer, his brow furrowed. "Just like with Hawthorne. But why a hospital this time?"

Morgan shook her head, frustration building. "I don't know. But look at the exit, Derik. Knox could have escaped, just like Hawthorne. But she didn't. Why?"

Ramirez cleared his throat. "There's more, Agent. A passerby reported hearing frantic screaming from inside about an hour ago. By the time first responders arrived..."

Morgan tried to piece together the gruesome puzzle. "So Knox was alive, panicking even, but didn't leave. What the hell happened in here?"

She knelt beside the body, careful not to contaminate the scene. Knox's face was frozen in an expression of terror, her eyes wide and staring. Morgan fought back a wave of nausea.

"This killer is escalating," she said, her voice low and tense. "The staging, the theme - it's all more elaborate. But the core is the same. He's giving his victims a chance to escape, but they can't. Or won't. We need to figure out why."

Morgan's gaze swept the surreal hospital setup, her mind struggling to process the grotesque tableau. The metallic scent of fear hung heavy in the air, mingling with the acrid odor of cheap disinfectant. She forced herself to focus on the details, cataloging each piece of evidence.

"The door was unlocked," she murmured, her voice barely audible over the hum of police activity. "Just like with Hawthorne. An escape route deliberately left open."

Derik stepped closer, his face grim. "But she didn't take it. Why?"

Morgan shook her head, frustration etching lines across her forehead. "That's the million-dollar question. According to the first responders, Knox was in a complete frenzy when they got here. Tearing the place apart, screaming..."

She trailed off, her eyes drawn to the overturned medical equipment, the scattered props. The scene told a story of desperation, of blind panic. Morgan could almost feel the terror that must have gripped Knox in her final moments.

"And then she just... collapsed," Morgan continued, her voice tight. "Died right here on the floor. But from what? There's no visible wound, no sign of physical trauma."

Derik ran a hand through his hair, his usual calm demeanor cracking under the weight of the scene. "Poison, maybe? Or some kind of drug?"

"Maybe," Morgan agreed, but her instincts were screaming that there was more to it. "We won't know for sure until we get the tox screen back. But whatever it was, it was fast-acting and devastating."

She turned away from the body, her eyes landing on the exit. The path to freedom that Knox had inexplicably ignored. "What was going through her mind?" Morgan wondered aloud. "What could possibly keep someone from escaping when the door was right there?"

The questions swirled in her mind, each one leading to another, none with satisfactory answers. Morgan took a deep breath, steeling herself. There was work to be done, and standing here speculating wouldn't get them any closer to catching this killer.

"Let's talk to the witness," she said to Derik, her voice regaining its professional edge. "Maybe he can shed some light on what happened here."

As they stepped outside, the pre-dawn chill hit Morgan like a physical force. Her eyes immediately found Gary, the man who had discovered Knox. He was leaning against a squad car, his body language screaming distress.

Morgan approached slowly, careful not to startle him. She'd dealt with traumatized witnesses before, knew how fragile their state of mind could be. Gary's hands were visibly shaking, his face ashen in the harsh glare of the police lights.

"Mr. Gary?" she said softly, keeping her tone gentle. "I'm Special Agent Cross. I know you've been through a lot tonight, but I was hoping we could talk for a moment."

Gary's eyes met hers, wide and haunted. Morgan felt a pang of sympathy. This man had walked into a nightmare, one that would likely stay with him for a long time to come.

"I... I tried to help her," Gary stammered, his voice barely above a whisper. "But she was just... screaming. Tearing everything apart. I've never seen anyone so terrified."

Morgan nodded encouragingly, her mind racing to connect the dots. "Can you tell me exactly what you saw when you entered the room?"

Gary took a shaky breath, his eyes unfocused as he relived the scene. "I was walking home from my night shift at the warehouse. It was so quiet, you know? Then I heard her screams. God, I've never heard anything like that before."

He paused, swallowing hard. Morgan waited patiently, giving him space to collect his thoughts.

"I thought someone was being attacked," Gary continued, his voice trembling. "So I ran to the door. It was unlocked. When I got inside, she was... she was like a wild animal. Throwing things, knocking stuff over. I tried to calm her down, but it was like she couldn't even see me."

Morgan nodded, her mind racing. The scene Gary described matched what they'd found inside, but it still didn't explain how Michelle Knox had died.

"Mr. Gary," Morgan said gently, "this is very important. Did you see anyone else nearby? Anyone at all?"

Gary shook his head emphatically. "No, ma'am. I was alone. Just me and her."

Morgan studied his face intently, searching for any hint of deception or uncertainty. But all she saw was genuine shock and distress. Gary's hands were still shaking, his eyes wide and haunted. He looked like a man who had stumbled into something far beyond his understanding.

As she observed him, Morgan felt a growing certainty that Gary was nothing more than an unfortunate bystander. His reaction was too raw, too visceral to be an act. Still, she couldn't shake the nagging feeling that something was missing from this picture.

"Thank you, Mr. Gary," she said softly. "You've been very helpful. We'll have someone take you home soon."

Morgan turned away from Gary, her brow furrowed in concentration. She walked back towards the crime scene, her eyes drawn to the darkened building looming before her. The flashing lights of police cruisers cast eerie, pulsing shadows across its facade.

"Something's not adding up," she muttered to herself, her voice barely audible above the low hum of activity around her.

Derik appeared at her side, his face grim. "What are you thinking?"

Morgan shook her head, frustration evident in her tense posture. "If Michelle had a way out, just like Hawthorne... why didn't she make it? What was different this time?" She turned to face her partner, her eyes intense. "The killer is escalating, Derik. They're choosing themes, creating scenarios. But what's the common thread?"

Derik ran a hand through his hair, equally perplexed. "Maybe it's not about the victims themselves, but what they represent?"

Morgan nodded slowly, her mind racing. "A courtroom for a judge, a hospital for..." She trailed off, realizing they didn't yet know Michelle Knox's occupation.

"We need to dig into Michelle's background," she said decisively. "Find out everything we can about her. There has to be a connection we're missing."

As they spoke, Morgan's gaze drifted back to the building. The staged hospital room inside seemed to mock her, a twisted puzzle box waiting to be solved. She could almost feel the killer's presence, lingering like a shadow just beyond her reach.

"One thing's for certain," she said, her voice low and determined. "They aren't finished yet. This is just the beginning of whatever sick game they're playing."

Derik nodded grimly. "So what's our next move?"

Morgan took a deep breath, steeling herself. "We work the scene, gather every scrap of evidence we can. Then we start connecting the dots. Hawthorne, Knox, the staging, the methods – there has to be a pattern. We just need to find it."

As she spoke, Morgan couldn't shake the feeling that they were running out of time. Somewhere out there, the killer was already planning their next performance. And she was determined to stop them before another innocent life was lost to this twisted spectacle.

CHAPTER TWELVE

The city skyline loomed ahead, a jagged silhouette against the first pale streaks of dawn. Morgan gripped the steering wheel tighter as she maneuvered through the empty streets, her eyes burning with exhaustion. Beside her, Derik stifled a yawn.

"You okay to do this?" he asked, concern lacing his voice.

Morgan nodded curtly. "We need answers. Sleep can wait."

As they pulled into the coroner's office parking lot, Morgan's mind raced. Two murders, both staged in bizarre settings. What was the connection? What was the killer trying to prove?

She pushed open the car door, wincing as her ankle twinged. The break had mostly healed, but reminders of that night in the woods with her father still lingered. Morgan shoved the memory aside. Focus on the case, she told herself sternly.

"Let's go," she said to Derik, leading the way into the building.

The familiar antiseptic smell hit them as soon as they entered, making Morgan's stomach churn. Or maybe that was just the lack of sleep and coffee. Dr. Emerson, the chief medical examiner, greeted them with bloodshot eyes and rumpled scrubs.

"Agents," he said, his voice gravelly. "Follow me."

As they trailed after him down the stark hallway, Morgan's unease grew. What would they find? What new horrors awaited them?

Dr. Emerson pushed open the door to the examination room. The harsh lights made Morgan squint as they stepped inside. Her gaze was immediately drawn to the sheet-covered form on the steel table.

"Before we begin," Dr. Emerson said, "I need to warn you. This isn't like anything I've seen before."

Morgan's pulse quickened. "What do you mean?"

The doctor's tired eyes met hers. "There are... anomalies. Things that don't add up."

"Such as?" Derik prompted.

Dr. Emerson took a deep breath. "Well, for starters—"

He was cut off by a loud crash from the hallway. They all whirled around as a young lab tech burst through the door, his face pale.

"Doctor! You need to see this right away!"

Dr. Emerson frowned. "What is it, Jenkins?"

The tech thrust a tablet towards him, hands shaking. "The toxicology results just came back. And there's something else we found during the examination. You're not going to believe this."

Morgan watched as Dr. Emerson's eyes widened, scanning the information on the screen. His face drained of color.

"My God," he whispered.

Morgan's heart pounded. "What? What is it?"

Dr. Emerson looked up, his expression grave. "Agents, I'm afraid we have two rather shocking revelations about Ms. Knox's death."

Dr. Emerson's words hung in the air, heavy with implication. Morgan leaned forward, her exhaustion momentarily forgotten as adrenaline surged through her veins.

"Tell us," she urged, her voice low and tense.

The coroner cleared his throat. "First, Michelle Knox was poisoned. But not just with any toxin. This was something rare, something I've never encountered before."

Morgan's brow furrowed. "What kind of poison are we talking about?"

"A carefully measured dose of a compound that caused a slow, systematic shutdown of her cardiovascular system," Dr. Emerson explained, his clinical tone belying the horror of his words. "It didn't kill her instantly. Instead, it... it allowed her to feel every excruciating moment as her body failed her."

Derik inhaled sharply. "Jesus Christ."

"So she was conscious? Aware of what was happening to her?"

Dr. Emerson nodded grimly. "Based on our findings, yes. Her heart would have weakened gradually, her lungs struggling for air. She likely experienced intense pain and panic in her final minutes alive."

The room fell silent as the full weight of this revelation settled upon them. Morgan's stomach churned, imagining Michelle's terror and suffering.

"The killer," Morgan mused aloud, her voice barely above a whisper, "he didn't need to restrain her. The poison did that for him."

Dr. Emerson's expression tightened. "That's... that's not all, Agent Cross. There's a second revelation that's equally disturbing."

Morgan braced herself. "Go on."

The coroner reached for a small evidence bag on the nearby tray. Inside was a tiny glass vial, its contents clear and innocuous-looking.

"This was found tucked away in the inner lining of Ms. Knox's blazer," he said, holding it up. "It's the antidote."

Morgan's eyes widened in disbelief. "What?"

"A small, tightly sealed vial containing the exact compound needed to counteract the poison," Dr. Emerson confirmed. "It was in her pocket the entire time."

Morgan stared at the vial, her mind reeling with the implications. The killer hadn't just murdered Michelle Knox. He had turned her death into a twisted game, a test she was doomed to fail.

"He gave her a chance," Morgan murmured, her voice thick with horror and anger. "He poisoned her, but left the cure right there with her. Why? What kind of sick bastard are we dealing with?"

Derik shook his head, his face ashen. "This isn't just murder. This is... psychological torture."

Morgan's fists clenched at her sides. The pieces were starting to fit together, forming a picture that chilled her to her core. This wasn't a simple killing. This was something far more calculated, far more sinister.

She turned to Derik, her eyes blazing with determination. "We need to dig deeper. There has to be a connection between Knox and Hawthorne. This killer, he's playing games. And I've got a feeling he's far from finished."

Morgan's gaze remained fixed on the small vial, her mind struggling to process the cruel irony of its presence. She could almost see Michelle Knox in her final moments, frantic and desperate, tearing apart the staged hospital room in search of salvation. The image made her stomach churn.

"She never even thought to check herself," Morgan said softly, her voice barely above a whisper. She looked up at Dr. Emerson, her eyes searching for confirmation. "The room was in disarray when we found her. She was looking for this, wasn't she?"

The coroner nodded grimly. "Based on the evidence, it appears Ms. Knox spent her final moments in a frenzied search. The toxicology report suggests she had about thirty minutes between ingestion and... the end."

Derik ran a hand through his hair, his face a mask of frustration. "Thirty minutes of terror, knowing you're dying, and the cure is right there in your pocket. It's beyond cruel."

Morgan's jaw clenched. She could feel the anger building inside her, a slow burn that threatened to consume her. "He wanted her to suffer," she said, her voice tight with controlled fury. "This wasn't just about killing her. It was about watching her struggle, fail, and die."

She turned away from the examination table, pacing the small room. "What kind of person does this? What's the point?"

Derik leaned against the wall, his arms crossed. "Maybe it's about power? Control? Proving something?"

Morgan stopped, her eyes narrowing as a thought struck her. "Or testing something," she murmured. She spun back to face her partner and the coroner. "Think about it. Both victims were given a chance, however slim. It's like... like he's running some sort of sick experiment."

Dr. Emerson cleared his throat. "Agent Cross, if I may... This level of planning, of psychological manipulation... You're not dealing with an ordinary killer here."

Morgan nodded, her expression grim. "No, we're not. And that's what scares me the most." She took a deep breath, steeling herself. "Because if this is some kind of test or experiment, then we can be damn sure he's not done yet."

Morgan's mind churned, piecing together the gruesome puzzle before them. She began to pace, her steps echoing in the quiet room. "Think about it," she said, gesturing with her hands as she spoke. "Judge Hawthorne, trapped in that makeshift courtroom. Michelle Knox, surrounded by fake hospital equipment. Both victims placed in staged settings, both given a way out."

"But neither made it," Derik added, his voice grim.

Morgan stopped pacing, turning to face her partner. "Exactly. Hawthorne's exit wasn't locked. If he'd been just a few seconds faster, he could have walked out alive." She paused, swallowing hard as she remembered the judge's body, so close to freedom. "And Michelle... her cure was in her own pocket. But in her panic, she never thought to check."

"Jesus," Derik muttered, running a hand through his hair. "What kind of monster does this?"

Morgan's eyes narrowed, her mind racing. "The kind that's not just killing for the sake of killing. He's testing them, Derik. But testing what?"

She resumed her pacing, her thoughts tumbling over each other. "Is it about their will to live? Their problem-solving skills under pressure? Or is it something else entirely?"

Derik pushed off from the wall he'd been leaning against. "Whatever it is, we need to figure it out fast. Because you're right,

Morgan. This isn't just murder. It's a game. And I've got a feeling we've only seen the opening moves."

Morgan took a slow, deliberate breath, her eyes scanning the sterile room as if the answers might materialize on the cold, tiled walls. The weight of responsibility pressed down on her shoulders, but she forced herself to focus, to think.

"This killer," she began, her voice barely above a whisper, "he's not just a murderer. He's fashioning himself as some sort of... twisted game master." She turned to Derik, her gaze intense. "He's creating trials, Derik. Forcing his victims to play by his rules, and when they fail..." She trailed off, the implications hanging heavy in the air.

Derik nodded grimly. "But why these two? What's the connection between a federal judge and an investment analyst?"

Morgan's brow furrowed as she considered the question. "That's what we need to figure out. On the surface, they seem worlds apart. Different circles, different lives." She began to pace, her mind racing. "But there has to be a link. Something that ties them together in the killer's mind."

"Could be professional," Derik offered. "Maybe Knox was involved in a case Hawthorne presided over?"

"Possible," Morgan mused, "but my gut tells me it's more than that. This feels... personal somehow."

She stopped pacing abruptly, turning to face her partner. "We need to dig deeper, Derik. Into both of them. Their histories, their connections, everything. Because now that we've confirmed the pattern—" She paused, the reality of what they were dealing with sinking in. "Now that we know this is the work of a serial killer, one thing's certain."

Derik met her gaze, understanding dawning in his eyes. "He's not finished," he said quietly.

Morgan nodded, a grim determination settling over her features. "Exactly. And we need to find the connection between Knox and Hawthorne before he strikes again." She reached for her coat, her movements decisive. "Let's head back to the office. We need to start combing through their lives, see if we can find any overlaps, any shared acquaintances, anything that might give us a clue as to why they were chosen."

CHAPTER THIRTEEN

The flickering blue light from the laptop screen cast eerie shadows across the dimly lit room, illuminating the man's expressionless face as he watched the news broadcast intently. His eyes, dark and unblinking, were fixed on the reporter's solemn visage as she delivered the latest update on the city's most shocking murder.

"Police are still investigating the brutal killing of Michelle Knox, the prominent real estate mogul found dead in her office late last night," the reporter announced, her voice grave. "Authorities are growing increasingly concerned that this may be the work of a serial killer," the reporter continued gravely. "This marks the second high-profile murder in as many days with strikingly similar MOs."

A slow, deliberate smile began to tug at the corners of the man's mouth. Serial killer. How quaint. How utterly simplistic. They had no idea of the true scope, the true purpose behind what he was doing.

His mind drifted back to Michelle Knox's final moments. He could picture it so clearly - her perfect manicure ruined as she clawed desperately at the set he'd created.

"All that time," he murmured to himself, savoring each word. "All that panic. And you never once thought to check your own pocket."

He chuckled softly, remembering how he had slipped the small envelope into her blazer. Such a simple thing, really. But in her blind terror, her desperate scramble for salvation, she had overlooked the obvious.

"How fitting," he mused aloud. "How utterly deserved."

It was poetic justice, really. Michelle Knox had built her empire on misdirection, on sleight of hand, on distracting people from what really mattered. And in the end, that very trait had been her undoing.

The killer interlaced his fingers, resting them gently on his abdomen as he reclined in the chair. His heartbeat remained slow and steady, a contrast to the frenzied rhythm that must have pounded in Michelle Knox's chest during her final moments. The world would call this murder, label him a monster, but he knew better. This was justice, pure and simple.

He closed his eyes, allowing a small smile to play across his lips. "They'll never understand," he murmured to himself, his voice barely above a whisper. "How could they? They're blind to the truth."

Opening his eyes, he leaned forward, focusing once more on the laptop screen. The news anchor's voice droned on, painting Michelle Knox as a tragic victim, a pillar of the community struck down in her prime.

He scoffed. "Pillar of the community," he repeated mockingly. "If only they knew."

Pushing back from the desk, he stood and began to pace the room, his movements deliberate and controlled. "Michelle Knox was no innocent victim," he said, his voice growing stronger with each word. "None of them are. They wrap themselves in the trappings of success, of power. Hide behind their fancy titles and carefully crafted reputations."

He paused, running a hand through his hair. "But I see them for what they truly are. Liars. Thieves. Destroyers of lives."

Turning back to the laptop, he studied Michelle Knox's smiling face on the screen. To the world, she had been a successful businesswoman, a philanthropist, a role model. But he knew the truth that lay beneath that carefully polished exterior.

"How many lives did you ruin, Michelle?" he asked the frozen image. "How many dreams did you crush? How many families did you tear apart with your greed?"

He leaned in close to the screen, his voice dropping to a whisper. "But now, you've faced true justice. And you're just the beginning."

His eyes drifted to a framed newspaper clipping on the wall, its headline bold and stark: "Judge Richard Hawthorne Found Dead." A faint smile tugged at the corners of his mouth as he approached it, fingers tracing the edge of the frame.

"Ah, Richard," he murmured, his voice a mix of contempt and satisfaction. "You were no different, were you?"

He plucked the frame from the wall, studying the stern face of the late judge. Hawthorne's eyes, even in newsprint, seemed to glare back at him with cold authority.

"Your death had nothing to do with your lofty position, did it?" he mused aloud, pacing slowly. "It wasn't about the black robe you wore or the gavel you wielded. No, it was about the man beneath all that pageantry."

He set the frame down on his desk, next to the laptop still displaying Michelle Knox's story. The juxtaposition of the two images seemed fitting.

"Cold," he spat, his voice rising. "Callous. Heartless. A man who made decisions without a shred of care for the lives he ruined."

His mind drifted back to Hawthorne's final moments, the fear in those once-imperious eyes. "And in the end, when faced with your own judgment, you failed spectacularly, didn't you, Richard?"

He chuckled, a sound devoid of warmth. "Just like Michelle. Just like all of them. When the tables turn, when they're the ones facing true justice, they all fail."

Abruptly, he shook his head, as if clearing away cobwebs of memory. "But there's no time for nostalgia," he muttered, his gaze hardening. "No time to dwell on past victories."

He turned back to his laptop, fingers hovering over the keyboard. "This is far from over," he whispered, a new fire lighting in his eyes. "Michelle, Richard - they were just the beginning."

As he began to type, plans forming with each keystroke, a grim smile spread across his face. The true work, he knew, was only just beginning.

CHAPTER FOURTEEN

The morning sun struggled against the thick glass of the FBI Headquarters, its rays reduced to a pale glow that barely touched the edges of the briefing room. Inside, the dawn's tentative light was an unwelcome contrast to the oppressive atmosphere hanging over the agents. Despite the new day, the air felt stale, fraught with the weight of sleepless nights and the pressure of the unsolved.

Morgan sat motionless at the table, save for the unconscious weave of her fingers through her tousled dark hair—a physical manifestation of her mind's relentless spinning. The case board before her was a battleground of facts and theories, red string zigzagging like scars across the evidence. On one flank, the stoic visage of Judge Richard Hawthorne; on the other, Michelle Knox's confident smile—two faces etched with the finality of their gruesome ends.

The similarities in their deaths taunted Morgan from the board. Both victims discovered alone, surrounded by theatrically staged scenes mocking their professions. Hawthorne's blood had painted a grotesque mural on his own private courtroom, while Knox's life ebbed away amidst the cold sterility of mock medical equipment. It was as if the killer aimed to underscore their careers with a twisted homage in death.

Morgan's gaze lingered on Hawthorne's image. A man vested with the power of judgment, now himself judged and executed in a parody of justice. And Knox—an arbiter of wealth whose decisive hand once played with the fortunes of many, found dead with the means of salvation so close yet tragically ignored.

She tried to pierce through the fog of information, seeking a thread to pull, a connection that might unravel the knot of this enigma. But the web was complex, and each potential link led only to more questions. The irony of it all wasn't lost on her—the killer was out there, weaving these intricate patterns, while she sat here, caught in her own tangle of clues and dead ends.

In the dim light of early morning, the photographs of the deceased seemed to whisper of secrets just beyond reach. Morgan knew better than to rely solely on legal logic. The law was black and white, but human motivation lived in the grey, and somewhere in that murky realm lay the answers she sought.

As the silence of the room wrapped around her, the memory of her father's words from their clandestine meeting in the woods resonated within her. John Christopher's revelation about Cordell's vendetta pulsed through her veins, mingling with the urgency of the current case. She couldn't shake the feeling that somehow, the shadow of Cordell's past actions reached even into this investigation, though the nature of that reach remained elusive.

Patiently, she waited for the spark of insight, the elusive glimmer of connection that would bring the killer's motives into stark relief. The stakes were personal, each victim a haunting echo of her own struggle against the injustice that had once consumed her life. She wouldn't rest until the killer was unmasked, until the sins of the past were laid bare for all to see.

Morgan's fingers stilled on the file she had been leafing through, her gaze locked on the clock above the case board. Hours had evaporated in their relentless pursuit of a connection between Judge Hawthorne and Michelle Knox. She felt Derik's presence like a steady pulse beside her, his own determination mirroring hers. The room had grown stale with the scent of old coffee and the recycled breath of two agents too stubborn to pause.

"Nothing," she muttered under her breath, shuffling through another stack of papers that held interviews, alibis, timelines. Each document was a silent testament to their failure to find the invisible thread that linked their victims. Derik leaned back, his chair creaking in protest, his green eyes scanning the room as if hoping the walls would yield an answer. They were both chasing ghosts through the labyrinth of evidence, and it was wearing thin on Morgan's resolve.

"Maybe we're looking at this wrong," Derik suggested, though Morgan could hear the weariness in his voice. He had shadows under his eyes that spoke of their shared vigil, and she knew he felt every bit of the exhaustion that clawed at her.

"Then we turn it inside out until it makes sense," she said, but the words sounded hollow even to her own ears. It was the mantra of the desperate, the creed of the sleep-deprived.

Without warning, her vision blurred, letters on the open file before her dancing into an indecipherable jumble. She blinked hard, pressing the heel of her hand against her forehead as if she could physically shove the fatigue aside. Her body was rebelling, nearly two full days without proper rest, sustained by a cocktail of caffeine and adrenaline that was losing its potency.

Morgan's fingers pressed into her temples, kneading the skin as if she could massage away the fatigue that clung to her like a second skin. The room around her was a blur of papers and photographs, the evidence board a constellation of red strings and thumbtacks that refused to align into any meaningful pattern. She felt the weight of every second of the near-forty-eight hours that had slipped by since her last real rest, each one heavy with the urgency of the case.

Meanwhile, Derik rifled through a fresh stack of documents, his movements methodic, almost mechanical. Then, without warning, he froze. The abrupt stillness drew Morgan's gaze, and she found herself locked onto him, her own exhaustion momentarily forgotten.

"Derik?" she prodded, her voice gravelly from overuse.

He looked up, and there it was—that flash of clarity in his eyes that she'd come to know so well. "Morgan," he began, the timbre of his voice cutting through the static of her tired mind, "I think we've been looking at this all wrong."

She leaned in, her weariness pushed aside by the sheer force of her resolve. "What do you mean?"

"Michelle Knox," he said, tapping a finger against a particular sheet of paper. "A few years back, a family tried to sue her under the state's bystander laws."

Morgan straightened in her seat, the fog in her brain dissipating just enough to let the implication of his words sink in. Bystander laws—the kind that addressed the moral duty of a person to intervene in an emergency.

"Go on," she urged, the cogs in her mind beginning to turn once again.

"Knox was accused of ignoring a man suffering a heart attack right in front of her," Derik continued. "The family claimed she just watched him die, that she had a responsibility to help, or at least call for help."

"And?" Morgan's heart quickened, sensing the tendrils of a connection starting to form.

"Case got thrown out. No legal obligation to act meant Knox walked free. But that family—they lost someone because she decided not to act. And now Knox is dead, in a scene staged like a hospital room, with lifesaving medicine just... out of reach."

The pieces clicked into place, a cold realization washing over Morgan. Michelle Knox, left to die with salvation so close yet ignored—just as she had done to that man. It was poetic, cruel justice, the kind that spoke of a meticulous and moralistic killer.

Morgan's frown deepened as she heard Derik recount the incident with a measured gravity that seemed to pull the air heavy around them. In the lobby of her opulent office building, Michelle Knox had been on her way to an important meeting when a crisis unfolded before her very eyes. A man, just an arm's length away, had collapsed, his hands clutching at his chest in silent horror. The onset of a heart attack was unmistakable.

As if caught within a tableau of indifference, Knox had glanced at the stricken figure and simply continued on her path without breaking stride. Morgan pictured the scene—bystanders frozen in shock, the man's anguished gasps fading into stillness, and Knox, whose life was governed by the ticking of a clock rather than the beating of a heart.

"Didn't even call for help," Derik added, flipping through the case details with a frustration that echoed Morgan's own. His voice held a note of disgust, a sentiment that clashed with the typically unflappable demeanor of his professional façade.

The family of the deceased had sought justice, their grief channeled into a lawsuit that accused Knox of failing to fulfill a moral responsibility that any decent human being would shoulder instinctively. But the law had no room for morality; it was cold, clinical. It stated that Knox had no duty to act, and the judge had concurred. Their case crumbled, and Knox walked free, untouched by the tragedy she'd dismissed with a callous gait.

"Law is one thing, humanity another," Morgan muttered, her words barely audible as they were absorbed by the thick carpet beneath her feet. She stared at the photographs and reports scattered across the table, each one a fragment of a puzzle that was slowly aligning itself within her weary mind.

"Exactly," Derik responded, sensing Morgan's train of thought. "It's not about whether it was legal. It's about whether it was right."

A sharp edge of clarity cut through Morgan's exhaustion. She knew too well how the tendrils of corruption could strangle justice, how the law could be manipulated and contorted until it served only those with the power to bend it. Her past, the years stolen from her by the very institution she served, had taught her the bitter lesson that justice and legality often traveled divergent paths. And now, it seemed, someone else understood that too—someone who dealt punishment where the law had failed.

"Derik," she said, her voice hoarse but resolute, "we're looking at someone who's not just killing. They're sending a message. We need to find out what message Hawthorne sent... or didn't."

Morgan's spine snapped to attention, her physiology betraying the fatigue that had clawed at her for hours. The room spun briefly as she sat up straighter, the weak morning light doing nothing to ease the shadows beneath her eyes. Her hands, adorned with traces of ink from years past, trembled faintly as her pulse quickened. It was a visceral reaction to an unspoken truth that gnawed at her conscience. Knox had passed by a dying man, her indifference as lethal as any weapon. It wasn't about what was legal. It was about what was right. And Hawthorne?

Her gaze swept across the table, coming to rest on another file, one that bore the name Sarah Reeves. The secretary-turned-law-clerk who had found peace—or so it seemed—in the embrace of death; a last resort to silence her despair. Morgan had initially dismissed Sarah's demise as a tragic coincidence, a thread dangling with no clear end in sight. But now, doubt crept into the crevices of her certainty, seeping through like water through cracked concrete.

The case file sat there, a silent testament to a life extinguished prematurely. As Morgan scanned the details once more, the facts danced mockingly before her. She could feel the walls of her resolve being chipped away with each sentence she reread. The suicide note, the meticulously arranged belongings, the untroubled history—all elements of a narrative she had categorized as irrelevant.

But something clawed at the back of her mind, insistent and impossible to ignore. Could she have been too quick to dismiss the significance of Sarah's death? If the killer's motive was rooted in moral judgment, retribution for sins not paid in the eyes of the law, then perhaps Sarah Reeves had been more than a casualty of her own war. Perhaps she had been a statement, a prologue to a series of orchestrated condemnations.

This new realization was a puzzle piece that Morgan hadn't even known she was missing. Yet here it was, fitting snuggly into place, making the image clearer, sharper, more horrifying. There was a pattern emerging, one that suggested a killer moving through a list of selected targets—not at random, but with deliberate intent. A vigilante who had taken upon themselves to be judge, jury, and executioner.

"Derik," she began, her voice barely above a whisper, yet heavy with implication, "what if Hawthorne ignored Sarah's cries for help, just as Knox did with that man?" She felt the weight of her own words settle in the room.

Derik turned his eyes away from the documents, their contents now secondary to the gravity in Morgan's tone. He knew that look, the one where her instincts were piecing together a larger, more sinister picture.

"Could be," he admitted, his brow furrowing. "We can't rule it out. Not with a pattern emerging."

The silence stretched between them, punctuated only by the quiet hum of fluorescent lights above.

A killer haunting the moral fringes, punishing those who had transgressed an unwritten code of ethics—it made a twisted kind of sense. Sarah Reeves's suicide, once a sorrowful footnote in Hawthorne's career, now glimmered with potential significance. It was a lead that demanded exploration, a path that could unravel the enigma of these calculated deaths.

"Sarah's family," Morgan said decisively, the fatigue that clung to her frame cast aside by the surge of adrenaline. "We need to talk to them." Her dark eyes locked onto Derik's, conveying an urgency that needed no further explanation.

"Let's do it," Derik agreed, standing up, ready to follow Morgan's lead.

Their journey would take them into the heart of Sarah's past, sifting through memories and secrets in search of the truth. There, they hoped to find the catalyst that sparked this lethal chain of events—to understand why Sarah died and to prevent the killer from exacting their brand of retribution on anyone else. Somewhere amidst the threads of Sarah's life lay the answer to the riddle that now consumed Morgan Cross, and she wouldn't rest until it was uncovered.

CHAPTER FIFTEEN

The pale morning sun cast an accusatory glare over the suburban landscape, as if nature itself was passing judgment on the secrets buried within these cookie-cutter homes. Morgan squinted against the harsh light, her eyes tracing the outline of Darren Reeves' modest house. It was unremarkable, save for the invisible weight of grief that seemed to hang over it like a shroud.

She glanced at Derik, noting the tension in his jaw. He'd been quiet on the drive over, and she knew he was still smarting from being shut out of her plans. But this wasn't the time to address that. They had a job to do.

"You ready?" she asked, her voice low.

Derik nodded, his green eyes meeting hers briefly before flicking away. "Let's do this."

The sound of approaching footsteps from within the house pulled her from her thoughts. She straightened, adopting the professional demeanor that had become second nature since her return to the Bureau.

The door swung open, revealing a man who looked like he'd aged a decade in a year. Darren Reeves stood before them, his face a map of sorrow. Dark circles ringed his hollow eyes, and his skin had a sickly pallor that spoke of sleepless nights and relentless grief.

Morgan felt a twinge of empathy, quickly suppressed. She couldn't afford to let emotion cloud her judgment. Not when they were so close to unraveling this case.

"Mr. Reeves?" she said, her tone carefully modulated. "I'm Agent Cross, and this is Agent Greene. We'd like to ask you a few questions about your sister, Sarah."

Darren's eyes widened slightly at the mention of Sarah's name, a flicker of pain crossing his features before he schooled them into a wary mask. "Why?" he asked, his voice rough with disuse. "It's been a year. Why are you here now?"

Morgan hesitated, weighing her words carefully. How much should she reveal? How much did Darren already know? She thought of Sarah's picture, smiling and full of life, contrasted with the broken man before her. The truth, she decided. Or at least, part of it.

"We believe your sister's death may be connected to a current investigation," she said, watching Darren's reaction closely. "We're hoping you might be able to provide some insight."

Darren's gaze darted between Morgan and Derik, his brow furrowing. She could almost see the wheels turning in his mind, weighing the risk of letting them in against the possibility of finally understanding why his sister was gone.

Finally, he stepped back, opening the door wider. "Come in," he said, his voice barely above a whisper. "But I don't know what I can tell you that I haven't already told the police."

As Morgan followed Darren into the house, she caught Derik's eye. There was a silent question there, a plea for inclusion. She gave him a small nod, a promise to fill him in later. For now, they had a grieving brother to interview and a case to crack.

Morgan stepped into the living room, her trained eyes immediately scanning the space. The house was immaculate, each surface polished to a shine, but there was an underlying emptiness that spoke volumes. It was as if grief itself had taken up residence, lurking in the corners and casting long shadows across the pristine floors.

Her gaze settled on a shelf by the fireplace, and her breath caught in her throat. There, nestled among various knick-knacks, was a framed photograph of Sarah Reeves. The young woman's smile was radiant, her eyes sparkling with a vitality that seemed to leap out of the frame. Morgan felt a pang in her chest, recognizing the contrast between the vibrant woman in the photo and the tragic end she had met.

"Your sister," Morgan said softly, nodding toward the picture. "She was beautiful."

Darren followed her gaze, his shoulders sagging as if the weight of his loss had suddenly become tangible. "She was," he replied, his voice thick with emotion. "That was taken about a year before... before it happened. She'd just gotten the clerkship with Judge Hawthorne. She was so excited, so full of hope."

Hawthorne. The same judge they'd found murdered in that bizarre mock courtroom. She glanced at Derik, seeing the same realization dawning in his eyes.

"Mr. Reeves," Morgan began, choosing her words carefully, "I know this is difficult, but could you tell us more about Sarah's time working for Judge Hawthorne? Did she ever mention any... unusual occurrences or concerns?"

As Darren sank into an armchair, Morgan perched on the edge of the sofa, leaning forward intently.

"I'm listening," she said gently, her tattooed hands clasped tightly in her lap. "Whatever you can tell us, no matter how small it might seem, could be crucial."

Darren's hands trembled as he rubbed them together, his gaze fixed on the carpet. Morgan watched him intently, noting the way grief seemed to have etched itself into the lines of his face.

"Sarah," he began, his voice barely above a whisper, "she loved that job at first. God, she was so excited." A ghost of a smile flickered across his lips. "She'd always been ambitious, you know? Worked her ass off in law school, determined to make something of herself."

Morgan nodded, encouraging him to continue. She could relate to that drive, that burning desire to prove oneself. It was what had kept her going through the darkest days of her wrongful imprisonment.

Darren's expression darkened. "But over time, something changed. The light in her eyes started to dim. She'd come home later and later, always looking... haunted."

Morgan leaned forward, her heart rate quickening. "What do you think caused that change, Mr. Reeves?"

Darren's jaw clenched. "Hawthorne," he spat the name like it left a bad taste in his mouth. "The man was brilliant, no doubt about that. A legal mind like no other. But he was cold. Ruthless."

Morgan exchanged a glance with Derik, who had been silently observing from his position near the fireplace. She could see the wheels turning in his mind, matching this description to what they knew of the murdered judge.

"How so?" Morgan prompted gently.

Darren's hands balled into fists. "He demanded perfection. Absolute, unwavering perfection. And Sarah... well, she was good. Too good, maybe. Once Hawthorne saw how capable she was, how efficiently she could handle his cases, he zeroed in on her."

Morgan felt a chill run down her spine. She'd seen that type before - the kind of person who recognized talent and exploited it mercilessly. "Did Sarah ever consider quitting?" she asked, already suspecting the answer.

Darren shook his head, a bitter laugh escaping him. "She should have. God, I begged her to. But Sarah... she was stubborn. Determined. She thought if she could just tough it out, prove herself..."

As Darren's voice trailed off, Morgan found herself lost in thought. She couldn't help but draw parallels between Sarah's situation and her own past. The pressure to prove oneself, the relentless pursuit of justice - it was a path that could easily lead to self-destruction if one wasn't careful.

"Mr. Reeves," Morgan said softly, "I know this is difficult, but anything else you can tell us about Judge Hawthorne and his relationship with Sarah could be crucial to our investigation."

Darren's eyes clouded with a mixture of anger and sorrow as he continued, his voice strained. "Sarah... she was drowning. Every night, she'd come home looking like she'd aged ten years. Dark circles under her eyes, hands shaking from too much coffee and not enough sleep."

Morgan leaned forward, her tattooed arms resting on her knees. She could almost see Sarah, a shadow of herself, stumbling through the door night after night.

"I begged her to quit," Darren said, his voice cracking. "Told her it wasn't worth destroying herself over. But she wouldn't listen. Said she had her eye on a promotion, that it was her ticket out."

"And Hawthorne denied it," Morgan finished, her jaw clenching.

Darren nodded, his hands balling into fists. "Not because she wasn't qualified. Hell, she was probably the most qualified person in that entire courthouse. No, he denied it because he didn't want to lose his grip on her. She was his perfect little workhorse, and God forbid she ever escape his control."

Morgan felt a surge of anger course through her veins. She'd seen this type before - men who used their power to crush those beneath them, to keep them small and controllable.

"Mr. Reeves," she said, her voice low and steady, "can you tell me about the last time you saw your sister? Anything at all might help."

Darren's face contorted, as if physically pained by the memory. "It was the day before... before she..." He swallowed hard, unable to finish the sentence. "I stopped by her office to try one last time to convince her to quit. She was at her desk, writing something. Hawthorne walked by, like he always did, making his rounds."

Morgan watched as Darren's grief swelled, his voice thickening with emotion. She could picture the scene - Sarah, hunched over her desk, pen in hand, the weight of her despair evident in every line of her body. And Hawthorne, cold and imperious, striding past without a care in the world.

"He saw what she was writing," Darren continued, his voice barely above a whisper. "I don't know what it was, but the look on his face... It was like he knew. He knew something was terribly wrong, and he just... kept walking."

Morgan felt a chill run down her spine. The pieces were starting to fall into place, a picture forming that was as tragic as it was infuriating. She glanced at Derik, seeing her own grim realization mirrored in his eyes.

Darren's voice cracked as he continued, his eyes glistening with unshed tears. "It was a suicide note. A desperate cry for help, right there in front of him. And that bastard just kept walking. Didn't say a word. Didn't ask if she was okay. Didn't stop."

Morgan's heart clenched, the weight of Darren's words settling heavily in her chest. She could picture Sarah, alone and desperate, pouring her pain onto the page while the very man who had pushed her to the brink simply ignored her suffering.

"That night," Darren whispered, his voice barely audible, "she took her own life."

The room fell silent, the gravity of the revelation hanging in the air like a physical presence. Morgan struggled to maintain her composure, her mind racing with the implications of what she'd just heard. She glanced at Derik, noting the tightness in his jaw, the way his hands gripped the arms of his chair.

Darren's hands clenched into fists, his knuckles turning white with the force of his grip. His voice trembled with a mixture of grief and rage as he forced out the words. "My sister might still be alive today—if someone had just cared enough to stop."

Morgan felt a surge of empathy for Darren, remembering her own losses, her own battles with those who should have cared but didn't. She leaned forward, her voice gentle but firm. "Darren, I can't imagine how painful this must be for you. But your sister's story, what happened to her... it might be the key to solving these murders."

Darren looked up, confusion mixing with the pain in his eyes. "Murders? What do you mean?"

Morgan hesitated, weighing how much to reveal. She caught Derik's eye, seeing him give a slight nod of encouragement. Taking a deep breath, she began to explain, carefully omitting any classified details. "We believe the person responsible for Judge Hawthorne's death may have been motivated by a desire for justice... or revenge."

As she spoke, Morgan couldn't help but wonder: Was this the connection she'd been searching for? A vigilante, punishing those who had the power to help but chose to do nothing? The thought sent a chill down her spine, even as it ignited a spark of hope that they might finally be on the right track.

"Darren," she said, her voice low and intense, "I know this is difficult, but I need to ask you something. Did your sister ever mention anything about Michelle Knox?"

Darren's brow furrowed. "Michelle Knox? I don't think so. Who is she?"

Morgan exchanged a quick glance with Derik before continuing. "She was an investment banker. Recently murdered." She paused, carefully choosing her next words. "Like Judge Hawthorne, she... she had an opportunity to help someone in need. And she chose not to."

Darren's eyes widened, a flicker of understanding crossing his face. "You think... you think there's a connection?"

Morgan nodded slowly, her mind still processing the implications. "It's possible. Both victims had the power to save a life, and both did nothing. They just... kept walking."

As she spoke the words aloud, Morgan felt a chill run down her spine. The parallel was undeniable, and it stirred something deep within her – a memory of her own past, of the injustice she'd faced, of those who had turned a blind eye when she needed help the most.

She thought of Richard Cordell, of the corrupt system that had stolen ten years of her life. Of Thomas, gunned down on that pier. Of her father, forced into hiding. All because people in power had chosen to look away, to keep walking when they should have stopped.

Morgan's jaw clenched, a familiar fire of determination igniting in her chest. This case wasn't just about solving murders anymore. It was about confronting a deeply rooted injustice, one that resonated with her own experiences in ways she was only beginning to understand.

She turned back to Darren, her voice steady despite the tumult of emotions swirling within her. "Thank you for sharing your sister's story with us. It might be more important than you realize."

CHAPTER SIXTEEN

Morgan's skull pounded. She blinked hard, fighting against the heaviness of her eyelids as she leaned over the scattered files on the briefing room table. The coffee in her mug had long since gone cold, a testament to how long she and Derik had been at this.

"We're missing something," Morgan muttered, more to herself than to Derik. Her fingers traced the edge of a photo, Linda Worth's grief-stricken face staring back at her.

Derik's chair creaked as he shifted. "Maybe we should take a break, get some fresh air."

Morgan shook her head, wincing at the movement. "No time. Two people are dead, Derik. We can't afford breaks."

She could feel his concerned gaze on her, knew he was cataloging the dark circles under her eyes, the slight tremor in her hands. But she couldn't let herself rest, not when the killer could be planning their next move.

"Morgan," Derik's voice was gentle. "You're no good to anyone if you run yourself into the ground."

She finally looked up, meeting his green eyes. The worry there made her chest ache. "I know," she admitted softly. "But every time I close my eyes, I see their faces. Hawthorne. Knox. I can't shake the feeling that we're already too late for the next victim."

Derik reached across the table, his fingers brushing hers. "We'll find them. We always do."

Morgan allowed herself a moment to draw strength from his touch before pulling away. She stood, stretching muscles stiff from hours of inactivity, and moved to the board where the Worths' photos were pinned.

"What do you make of them?" she asked, studying Carl Worth's face. There was something in his eyes, a hint of barely contained rage that made her skin prickle.

Derik joined her at the board. "Grieving family, failed lawsuit. It's a common enough story."

"But not a quiet one," Morgan mused, tapping her finger against Carl's photo. "The way they went after Knox... it was personal."

"You think they might be involved?"

Morgan shrugged, frustration bubbling up. "I don't know. But right now, they're our best lead."

She turned back to the table, rifling through the files until she found what she was looking for. "Here," she said, holding up a document. "The transcript from the lawsuit dismissal. The language Carl Worth used... it was volatile."

Derik took the paper, his brow furrowing as he read. "Sounds like he had a hard time accepting the judge's decision."

"Wouldn't you?" Morgan asked, her voice low. "If someone walked past your dying brother and faced no consequences?"

The question hung in the air between them, heavy with unspoken weight. Morgan knew Derik was thinking of his own estranged son, of the bridges burned by his past mistakes.

Morgan's eyes narrowed as she studied the transcript, her mind replaying the courtroom scene. The words seemed to leap off the page, Carl Worth's rage palpable even through the cold, clinical text.

"Linda filed the lawsuit," Morgan murmured, her voice rough with fatigue, "but Carl... he was the one who couldn't contain himself."

Derik leaned in, his shoulder brushing against hers. The familiar warmth of his presence steadied her, even as exhaustion threatened to drag her under. "What exactly did he say?"

Morgan's finger traced the line on the page. "When the case was dismissed, he shouted at Michelle Knox. His exact words were: 'You'll still pay for what you did.'"

She looked up, meeting Derik's concerned gaze. The weight of those words hung between them, heavy with implication.

"A threat," Morgan said, her voice barely above a whisper.

Derik nodded, his green eyes darkening. "Or a promise."

They exchanged a look, years of partnership allowing them to communicate without words. Morgan felt a surge of adrenaline cut through her exhaustion, her mind snapping into focus.

"We need to talk to Carl Worth," she said, already pushing herself to her feet. "Now."

Derik didn't argue, grabbing his jacket from the back of his chair. "I'll drive. You look like you're about to collapse."

Morgan wanted to protest, but the room swam slightly as she stood. She gritted her teeth, forcing herself to stay upright. "I'm fine."

"Sure you are," Derik muttered, but his hand was gentle on her elbow as he steadied her.

As they moved towards the door, Morgan's mind raced. Could Carl Worth be their killer? The timing fit, the motive was there, but something niggled at the back of her mind. It felt too... neat. Too obvious.

"What are you thinking?" Derik asked as they stepped into the elevator.

Morgan leaned against the wall, closing her eyes briefly. "I'm thinking we're missing something. Carl's outburst... it's the kind of lead that looks good on paper, but..."

"But your gut's telling you otherwise," Derik finished for her.

She nodded, opening her eyes to find him watching her intently. "Yeah. But right now, it's all we've got. And if I'm wrong..."

"If you're wrong, we might prevent another murder," Derik said firmly. "We have to check it out."

The elevator doors opened, and they stepped out into the parking garage. As they walked to Derik's car, Morgan felt the weight of her exhaustion, the pressure of the case, and the ever-present shadow of her own past pressing down on her. But beneath it all, there was a spark of determination. They would find this killer, no matter what it took.

***

Morgan's eyes swept over the modest single-story house before her, taking in every detail. The neatly trimmed lawn, its blades of grass standing at perfect attention, seemed to mock the chaos of her own life. The freshly painted porch gleamed in the afternoon sun, its pristine white conflicting with the darkness of the case that had brought them here.

As she and Derik approached the front door, Morgan noticed the curtains in the front window stirring gently in the breeze. It was all so... normal. So innocuous. The kind of place you'd expect to find a friendly neighbor, not a potential murderer.

"Doesn't exactly scream 'psychopath's lair,' does it?" she murmured to Derik.

He shook his head, his expression grim. "They never do."

Morgan raised her hand to knock, but hesitated for a moment. "What if we're wrong about this, Derik? What if we're chasing the wrong lead while the real killer is out there planning their next move?"

Derik's hand squeezed her shoulder briefly. "We follow every lead, Morgan. That's the job."

She nodded, steeling herself, and rapped sharply on the door. For a long moment, there was silence. Then, the sound of footsteps approaching.

The door swung open, and Morgan found herself face to face with Carl Worth. Her breath caught in her throat. The man before her looked nothing like the enraged figure she'd seen in the courtroom photos. This Carl Worth seemed... diminished. Older than his years, his face lined with a grief that had settled into something quiet but permanent.

"Can I help you?" he asked, his voice rough with disuse.

Morgan cleared her throat. "Mr. Worth? I'm Agent Cross, and this is Agent Greene. We're with the FBI. We'd like to ask you a few questions if that's alright."

Carl's eyes flickered between them, a shadow of something—pain? fear?—passing over his features. For a moment, Morgan thought he might refuse them entry. But then his shoulders sagged, and he stepped back, gesturing them inside.

As they followed him into a living room that smelled faintly of lemon furniture polish and old books, Morgan couldn't shake the feeling that they were missing something crucial. The pieces of the puzzle were there, she was sure of it. But how they fit together... that was still frustratingly out of reach.

Carl Worth's eyes darkened as he caught sight of their badges, his jaw clenching visibly. Morgan tensed, ready for hostility, but as she explained their presence, something in Carl's expression shifted. The anger drained away, replaced by a weariness that seemed bone-deep.

"Michelle Knox," he murmured, sinking into an armchair. "I heard about what happened to her on the news. Terrible business."

Morgan studied him, her instincts on high alert. "Mr. Worth, we understand you had a... history with Ms. Knox. We need to ask you about your whereabouts during the time of her murder."

Carl didn't flinch. He met her gaze steadily, his voice calm as he replied, "I was at my sister-in-law's house. Linda's. We were going through some of my brother's old things. She can confirm it."

As Carl continued to answer their questions without hesitation, providing a solid alibi for both murders, Morgan felt a growing sense of unease. This wasn't the reaction she'd expected. Where was the bitterness, the lingering resentment?

"Mr. Worth," she probed, leaning forward slightly, "can you tell us about your brother? About what happened with Ms. Knox?"

Something flickered in Carl's eyes—not anger, but a deep, abiding sorrow. "My brother was a good man," he said softly. "What happened to him... it was senseless. Cruel. For a long time, I couldn't understand how someone could just walk by, ignore a person in need like that."

Morgan's pulse quickened. This was it—the moment of revelation she'd been waiting for. But Carl's next words caught her off guard.

"But blaming her... it didn't bring him back. It didn't change anything. I had to learn to let go of that anger, or it would have consumed me."

As Carl spoke about his brother, his voice steady and filled with a quiet acceptance, Morgan felt her certainty crumble. This wasn't the vengeful relative she'd expected to find. This was a man who had faced his grief and come out the other side.

She glanced at Derik, seeing her own surprise mirrored in his eyes. They'd been so sure, but now... Now, they were back at square one, with a killer still on the loose and no leads to follow.

Carl's gaze drifted to a framed photo on the mantle—a smiling man who bore a striking resemblance to him. His brother. He turned back to Morgan and Derik, his eyes glistening with unshed tears.

"I went to therapy," he admitted, his voice barely above a whisper. "It took time, but I learned to accept that my brother's death wasn't Michelle Knox's fault. She made a terrible choice that day, but she didn't cause his heart attack."

Morgan leaned forward, her tattooed arms resting on her knees. She studied Carl's face, searching for any hint of deception. But all she saw was a man who had walked through fire and come out transformed.

"Mr. Worth," she said, her voice gentler than before, "can you tell us more about how you came to terms with what happened?"

Carl nodded slowly. "It wasn't easy. There were days I wanted to scream, to lash out at the world. But my therapist helped me see that holding onto that anger was only hurting me."

He paused, taking a deep breath before continuing. "I hated her for a long time. But I let it go. What would revenge even do for me?"

His words hung in the air, heavy with the weight of hard-won wisdom. Morgan felt a twinge in her chest, an echo of her own struggle with the desire for vengeance against those who had framed her.

She watched Carl closely, her trained eyes picking up every micro-expression, every subtle shift in his body language. But there was no trace of the man who had once raged in a courtroom. This Carl Worth had made peace with his loss.

"It sounds like you've come a long way," Morgan said, her voice carrying a hint of admiration.

Carl nodded, a sad smile touching his lips. "I have. It's not always easy, but I've learned to live with my loss. My brother wouldn't have wanted me to waste my life on bitterness and revenge."

***

The car's engine hummed softly as Morgan leaned her head against the cool glass of the passenger window. The world outside blurred into a hazy smear of colors, mirroring the fog that seemed to have settled over her mind. Two days without sleep was taking its toll, and Morgan could feel exhaustion pulling at her like quicksand.

"You okay?" Derik's voice cut through the silence, concern etched in his tone.

Morgan turned to look at him, her eyes heavy. "Just tired. Nothing a gallon of coffee won't fix."

Derik frowned. "Maybe you should catch some sleep when we get back to the office. I can handle the paperwork."

"No," Morgan shook her head, wincing at the dull ache the movement caused. "We can't afford to waste time. This killer-"

Her words trailed off as something tugged at the edges of her consciousness. A stray thought, elusive as smoke, danced just out of reach. Morgan closed her eyes, trying to grasp it.

"Morgan?" Derik's voice sounded distant.

The pieces began to fall into place, slowly at first, then with increasing speed. Carl Worth, his anger tempered by time and therapy. The raw grief in his eyes, softened but still present. The way he spoke about letting go, about the futility of revenge.

Morgan's eyes snapped open, adrenaline surging through her veins, pushing back the fog of exhaustion.

"Oh God," she breathed, her heart racing. "I might know who it is."

CHAPTER SEVENTEEN

Dr. Thomas Bryant sank into his favorite leather armchair, relishing the rare quiet of an empty house. No patients to see, no hospital rounds, no urgent calls—just blessed solitude. He closed his eyes, savoring the moment.

"I should be relaxing," he muttered, a wry smile tugging at his lips. But relaxation had never come easily to Thomas. Even on his days off, his mind raced with unfinished tasks and looming responsibilities.

His gaze drifted to the basement door. The unfinished renovation project lurked below, a constant reminder of his overpacked schedule. With a sigh, he heaved himself out of the chair.

"Might as well make some progress," he decided. "Sandra will be thrilled if I actually finish something around here for once."

Thomas retrieved his toolbox from the hall closet, the familiar weight oddly comforting in his hand. As a surgeon, he was used to precision instruments, but there was something satisfying about these rougher tools.

He pulled open the basement door, flicking on the light switch. The narrow wooden staircase creaked under his feet as he descended. The air grew noticeably cooler, carrying the faint scent of dampness.

Thomas wrinkled his nose. "Really need to get a dehumidifier down here," he mused.

At the bottom of the stairs, he surveyed the unfinished space. Bare concrete floors, exposed beams, and stacks of building materials greeted him. Half-completed drywall lined one wall where he'd started and abandoned the project weeks ago.

"Where did I leave off?" Thomas muttered, setting down his toolbox. He ran a hand through his salt-and-pepper hair, trying to recall his renovation plans.

The basement was meant to be a surprise for Sandra—a cozy den where they could unwind after long hospital shifts. But between emergency surgeries and board meetings, Thomas had barely made a dent in the work.

He sighed heavily. "I'm a better doctor than I am a handyman, that's for sure."

Still, he was determined to make progress today. Thomas rolled up his sleeves and picked up a piece of drywall, measuring it against the exposed studs.

As he worked, his mind drifted to his patients, upcoming procedures, the staff meeting next week. He shook his head, forcing himself to focus on the task at hand.

"One afternoon," he told himself firmly. "I can give Sandra one afternoon of undivided attention on this project."

But even as he said the words, Thomas knew it was a losing battle. His work was his life—it always had been. Sandra understood that about him, even if she wished it were different sometimes.

He cut the drywall, aligning it carefully against the wall. For now, at least, he could pretend to be just a regular guy working on his basement. Not Dr. Thomas Bryant, renowned surgeon with lives depending on him. Just Thomas, husband trying to do something nice for his wife.

The pretense was oddly comforting, even if it wouldn't last.

Thomas reached for his toolbox, the familiar weight of it grounding him in the present moment. As he set it down on the workbench, a faint rustling sound tickled the edge of his hearing. He froze, his hand still on the toolbox handle.

"Hello?" he called out, his voice echoing in the unfinished space. No response came.

Thomas shook his head, chuckling at his own jumpiness. "Get it together, Bryant. You're not in the OR now."

But as he turned back to his work, an inexplicable chill ran down his spine. The air in the basement seemed to shift, growing heavier, more oppressive. Thomas's analytical mind raced, trying to make sense of the sudden unease gripping him.

"It's just the dampness," he muttered, attempting to rationalize the feeling. "I really need to look into better ventilation down here."

He had barely finished the thought when a powerful arm clamped around his chest, pinning his arms to his sides. Thomas's surgeon's instincts kicked in, his body reacting before his mind could fully process what was happening.

"What the—" he began to shout, but a cloth pressed firmly over his nose and mouth, cutting off his words. The smell was sickeningly sweet, cloying, and instantly recognizable to his medical brain. Chloroform.

Thomas thrashed wildly, his elbow connecting with something solid behind him. He heard a grunt of pain, but the iron grip didn't loosen. His mind raced, cataloging his options, assessing his chances of escape with the cold precision he usually reserved for triage situations.

But even as he fought, Thomas could feel his limbs growing heavier, his thoughts becoming sluggish. The chemical was working with brutal efficiency, overriding his desperate attempts to stay conscious.

"No," he tried to say, but the word came out as little more than a muffled groan against the cloth. His vision began to darken at the edges, the basement fading into a swirling haze of shadows.

Thomas's last coherent thought was of Sandra. Would she come home to find the basement empty, tools abandoned, her husband vanished without a trace? The guilt of leaving her to face that horror alone was almost worse than the fear of what awaited him in the encroaching darkness.

As consciousness slipped away, Thomas felt himself being dragged backward, away from the safety of his home and into an abyss of terrifying uncertainty.

***

Consciousness returned to Dr. Thomas Bryant like a tide of icy water, shocking his system back to alertness. His head throbbed with a dull, persistent ache, each pulse of pain threatening to split his skull. He tried to swallow, but his mouth felt like it was stuffed with cotton, his tongue thick and uncooperative. As awareness crept back, a new sensation made itself known—a sharp, radiating ache from his shoulders, his arms pulled taut behind him.

Handcuffs. The realization hit him with a jolt of panic.

Thomas forced his eyes open, blinking rapidly to clear the fog from his vision. What he saw made his blood run cold, a chill racing down his spine despite the sweat beading on his forehead.

"What in God's name...?" he muttered, his voice a hoarse whisper.

He was seated at a table, but this was no ordinary dining room. The space around him was a bizarre facsimile of a high-end restaurant, every detail meticulously arranged yet somehow fundamentally wrong. Dim, golden light cast long shadows across carefully set tables, the warm glow at odds with the clammy fear gripping Thomas's heart.

His medical training kicked in, urging him to assess, to understand. "Think, Thomas," he coached himself. "What do you see?"

His gaze darted around the room, taking in the unsettling details. The tables were set with fine china and gleaming silverware, but there wasn't a single mark of use on any of them. At the far end, a bar stretched along the wall, bottles neatly arranged on glass shelves. But as he squinted, Thomas noticed the labels were peeling, the bottles dusty and untouched.

A mechanical voice crackled to life, emanating from unseen speakers. The sudden intrusion of sound made Thomas flinch, his handcuffs rattling against the chair.

"Dr. Bryant," the robotic voice intoned, devoid of any human inflection. "The air in this room will soon fill with carbon monoxide."

Thomas's breath caught in his throat, his medical training immediately supplying him with the gruesome details of what carbon monoxide poisoning would do to his body. He struggled to maintain his composure, fighting against the rising panic.

"Why are you doing this?" he called out, his voice hoarse. "What do you want from me?"

The mechanical voice continued, ignoring his questions. "The key to your escape is in front of you."

Thomas's eyes darted forward, scanning the table before him. There, set in the center, was a massive bowl of steaming food. The pungent aroma wafted towards him, a bizarre contrast to the sterile, artificial environment.

"Your salvation lies within," the voice added, a hint of cruel amusement coloring the synthesized tones.

Thomas stared at the bowl, his mind racing. The key was inside the food? He tugged at his restraints, the metal biting into his wrists. He couldn't use his hands. The realization hit him like a punch to the gut – they wanted him to eat his way to freedom.

"This is insane," he muttered, sweat beading on his forehead. "You can't expect me to—"

"The clock is ticking, Doctor," the voice interrupted. "I suggest you start soon if you wish to survive."

Thomas closed his eyes, trying to steady his breathing. He was a man of science, of careful procedures and sterilized environments. The thought of burying his face in that bowl, desperately searching for a key with his mouth, made his stomach churn.

But as he felt the air growing heavier, an acrid taste beginning to coat his tongue, he knew he had no choice. With a deep breath, Thomas leaned forward, his face hovering over the steaming bowl.

As Thomas's face hovered inches from the steaming bowl, a sudden flash of memory struck him with such force that he jerked back, nearly toppling the chair.

"I know why," he gasped, his voice barely above a whisper. "I know why I'm here."

The realization hit him like a freight train, transporting him back three years to a sunny afternoon in Dallas. He and Sarah had been celebrating their anniversary, indulging in a romantic getaway filled with wine, pasta, and leisurely strolls through cobblestone streets.

"Sarah," Thomas murmured, his wife's name a prayer on his lips. How different things had been then, how carefree and unburdened. Until that fateful dinner.

The memory unfolded with cruel clarity. They had been seated at a quaint trattoria, the warm Italian sun casting long shadows across their table. The air had been thick with the scent of garlic and herbs, the chatter of fellow diners a pleasant backdrop to their meal.

Then, chaos erupted.

"Help!" A woman's panicked cry pierced the air. "Someone, please help!"

Thomas's head snapped up, his fork clattering to the plate. Across the restaurant, a man in his sixties was on his feet, his face turning an alarming shade of purple. His hands clawed at his throat, eyes wide with terror.

"He's choking," Sarah gasped, gripping Thomas's arm. "Thomas, you have to do something!"

He froze, the weight of the situation crushing down on him. His medical training screamed at him to act, to rush over and perform the Heimlich maneuver. It would be simple, routine even. He had done it countless times before.

But fear, insidious and paralyzing, kept him rooted to his chair.

"I... I can't," he choked out, his voice barely audible over the commotion. “I just can't."

Thomas’s hands trembled as he gripped the edge of the table, his knuckles turning white. The malpractice lawsuit that had been hanging over his head for months flashed through his mind, a constant specter threatening to destroy everything he had worked for.

"Thomas, please!" Sarah's voice was desperate, her eyes darting between her husband and the choking man.

He shook his head, shame burning in his chest. "I'm not licensed here. If something goes wrong..." The words tasted bitter on his tongue, excuses that couldn't mask the truth of his cowardice.

A waiter rushed past their table, shouting in rapid Italian. Thomas watched, his heart pounding, as another diner leapt to his feet and hurried to the choking man's side. The would-be rescuer wrapped his arms around the victim's midsection, attempting the Heimlich maneuver with clumsy, panicked movements.

"It's not working," Sarah whispered, her voice choked with tears.

Thomas knew she was right. The man's technique was off, his thrusts too high and lacking the necessary force. He could see it all with agonizing clarity, knowing exactly what needed to be done.

But still, he sat.

The choking man's struggles grew weaker, his face now a terrifying shade of blue. Thomas's medical mind supplied the clinical details – hypoxia setting in, brain damage imminent.

"I can't watch this," Sarah said, burying her face in her hands.

Thomas couldn't look away. He cataloged every detail, every failed attempt at rescue, every agonizing second that ticked by. When the man finally collapsed to the floor, Thomas knew it was too late.

The restaurant erupted into chaos – screams, sobs, frantic calls for an ambulance. But Thomas heard it all as if from a great distance, the sounds muffled by the roaring in his ears.

"Is he...?" Sarah asked, her voice small and trembling.

Thomas nodded, unable to speak. He had just watched a man die, knowing he could have saved him. The weight of that knowledge settled over him like a shroud, suffocating in its intensity.

In the days that followed, as they cut their vacation short and returned home, Thomas scoured the local news. He waited for questions, for accusations, for someone to point a finger at the American doctor who had sat idle while a man died.

But nothing came. No legal repercussions, no professional consequences. He had escaped unscathed.

Yet the memory haunted him, surfacing in nightmares and quiet moments. The man's face, contorted in fear and desperation, was seared into his mind. Thomas knew he would carry this burden for the rest of his life, a constant reminder of the moment he had chosen self-preservation over his sworn duty to heal.

Thomas stared at the steaming bowl before him now, his heart hammering against his ribs. The scent of rich spices wafted up, a cruel mockery of fine dining. His stomach churned, not from hunger, but from the twisted irony of his situation.

"You want me to eat this?" he said aloud, his voice hoarse. "To choke myself, just like—" The words caught in his throat.

The mechanical voice crackled again. "Justice demands symmetry, Doctor. Dig in."

Thomas's mind raced, memories of that fateful night in the restaurant flooding back. The man's desperate gasps, the panicked faces of other diners. His own cowardice.

"I can't," he whispered, more to himself than his unseen captor. "I won't."

A bitter laugh escaped him. Here he was again, faced with a choice between self-preservation and doing the right thing. But this time was different. This time, there was no reputation to protect, no lawsuit to fear. There was only the crushing weight of his past mistakes.

"No," Thomas said, louder this time. His voice grew stronger with each word. "I won't play your sick game."

With a surge of desperate energy, he threw himself forward. His shoulder connected with the bowl, sending it flying off the table. The crash of shattering ceramic filled the room, followed by the wet splatter of food hitting the floor.

Thomas's chair teetered precariously, and for a moment, he thought he might topple over. He steadied himself, panting heavily, eyes fixed on the mess before him.

"Is this what you wanted?" he shouted into the empty room. "Another spectacle of human suffering?"

Silence answered him. Thomas strained against his bonds, the metal of the handcuffs biting into his wrists. The key was out there somewhere, hidden in the wreckage of his defiance.

As the acrid scent of carbon monoxide began to fill his nostrils, Thomas realized that his act of rebellion might have just sealed his fate. But for the first time in years, he felt a flicker of something that had long been absent – not hope, exactly, but a grim satisfaction in finally choosing action over inaction.

Thomas gritted his teeth, his muscles tensing as he prepared for what he knew would be a painful maneuver. With a sharp intake of breath, he twisted his body violently to the side, throwing his weight against the chair's unstable legs.

The world tilted abruptly. For a suspended moment, Thomas felt weightless, then gravity reasserted itself with brutal efficiency. He crashed to the floor, the impact reverberating through his bones and jarring his teeth. Pain exploded in his shoulder and hip where they connected with the hard surface.

"Damn it," he hissed through clenched teeth, fighting against the wave of dizziness that threatened to overwhelm him. His face pressed against the cold, sticky floor, a mixture of spilled food and his own sweat creating a nauseating cocktail beneath his cheek.

Ignoring the throbbing ache in his body, Thomas forced himself to focus. He had to find that key. His fingers, numb from the tight handcuffs, scrabbled desperately across the floor, searching for anything that might be his salvation.

"Come on, come on," he muttered, his voice barely above a whisper. Each second that ticked by felt like an eternity, the weight of his past choices pressing down on him as surely as the toxic air filling his lungs.

As he pushed aside chunks of broken ceramic, wincing as a shard sliced into his cheek, Thomas's thoughts raced. Was this truly justice for his inaction years ago? Or was it merely cruel revenge enacted by someone who couldn't understand the complexities of his situation?

"I didn't want anyone to die," he said aloud, his words directed at both his unseen captor and the ghost of the man he'd failed to save. "I was scared. I was selfish. But this... this isn't right either."

His breath came faster now, each inhalation more labored than the last. The carbon monoxide was working its insidious magic, slowly robbing him of oxygen. Dark spots danced at the edges of his vision, and a heaviness settled in his chest.

Thomas's movements became more frantic, his search more desperate. Blood trickled down his face from the cut on his cheek, mingling with the sweat and grime on the floor. He could feel his strength ebbing, his chances slipping away with each passing second.

"Please," he whispered, a prayer to any power that might be listening. "I can't die like this. Not without making it right."

And then, just as despair threatened to consume him, his fingers brushed against something cool and metallic. The key.

CHAPTER EIGHTEEN

Morgan leaned forward in the stiff-backed chair of the FBI briefing room, her fingers splayed across countless crime scene photographs and witness statements. The clock on the wall ticked away, indifferent to the urgency that thrummed through her veins. It was late afternoon, and shadows began to creep over the piles of evidence that had become the landscape of her obsession. She'd been here for hours, the same questions circling like vultures in her mind.

With a hand calloused from years of bearing the weight of her own past, she shuffled through the papers once more, seeking the elusive thread that would unravel the mystery. Then, amidst the sea of facts and conjecture, it surged forth—a stark realization so potent it struck her with the force of a physical blow. Darren Reeves. How had she missed it? His eyes had held sorrow, yes, but behind that veil of grief, there must have been something darker, something she'd failed to see.

In every meeting, Darren had played the part of the bereft sibling to perfection. His voice had cracked with emotion as he recounted Sarah's tragic end; his body had seemed to sag under the weight of loss. Not once had Morgan considered him capable of orchestrating the horrors that unfolded since. But now, hindsight sharpened her vision, and she saw the performance for what it was—a mask.

Her stomach churned, the bile of realization rising in her throat. He hadn't appeared vengeful or methodical—hadn't fit the profile of someone driven by rage to meticulously plan and execute such chilling retribution. Yet here she was, staring at the connection she should have made days ago. It was all there in front of her: Richard Hawthorne and Michelle Knox, both guilty of turning a blind eye when it mattered most, both punished with poetic cruelty. And who knew that pain better than Darren?

Morgan rose from her chair, her movements robotic as she gathered the files. Every fiber of her being screamed that time was slipping away, that Darren Reeves was out there, weaving his web of judgment around the next victim. She felt sick, the sickness of one who knows they've unwittingly allowed a monster to walk free, disguised as a victim. Her dark brown hair, usually a shield of professionalism, hung limply around her tattoo-covered arms, a testament to the weariness that had settled deep within her bones.

The air in the briefing room felt thick, suffocating. She needed to act, to move—to chase down the truth she'd so narrowly brushed past. But for just a moment, she stood still, allowing the gravity of her oversight to sink in fully before she set out to make it right. Darren Reeves was no longer just a grieving brother; he was the key to a door Morgan had never thought to open. And beyond that door lay a darkness she was now compelled to confront.

Morgan's heart hammered against her ribcage, an erratic drumline that echoed the blare of sirens as she and Derik raced through the streets of Dallas. The midday heat was oppressive, a thick blanket smothering the city, but inside the car, a chill had settled over Morgan. It was a cold realization, one that should have been obvious from the start: Darren Reeves, the trauma nurse. A man intimately acquainted with life and death, who knew how to keep someone alive just as well as he knew how to watch them die.

She thought of Carl Worth's brother, collapsing in the lobby, a life slipping away amidst the indifference of passersby—indifference personified by Michelle Knox. Darren Reeves had been there, hands determined and steady, fighting a losing battle against the shroud of death. And when his efforts weren't enough, when the man's breath faded into nothingness, Michelle Knox had continued on her path, unshaken, unbothered. It was a moment that seared itself into Darren's soul, a wound that never closed, festering into the vendetta that now consumed him.

"Are you okay?" Derik asked, casting a sidelong glance at her. His green eyes searched for reassurance, but what could she offer? She was chasing ghosts, haunted by the specters of her past and the looming threat of the present.

"I'm fine," she lied, her voice steadier than she felt. "Just focus on driving."

As they turned onto Darren's street, a foreboding silence swallowed the sirens' cries. Derik killed the lights, coasting the last few yards, their arrival as stealthy as a whisper. Morgan's fingers tightened around the handle of her gun, the metal cool and familiar in her palm. She glanced at Derik, seeing the same tension mirrored in his posture, the readiness that came with years of experience.

"Be careful," he murmured, his hand brushing against hers before they stepped out of the car. The world seemed to hold its breath, the only sound the crunch of gravel beneath their feet as they approached the house.

The front door loomed before them, a barrier to the truth that lay within. Morgan's mind raced with possibilities, each more grim than the last. What if they were too late? What unspeakable scene awaited them behind the mundane facade of suburbia?

With a nod from Derik, Morgan reached out and rang the doorbell. The hollow chime felt like a final plea for normalcy, a hope that maybe, just maybe, they were wrong about Darren Reeves. But the silence that followed spoke volumes, and Morgan's gut twisted with dread. This was no longer just a race against a killer; it was a descent into the heart of darkness, a journey she knew all too well.

"Ready?" Derik whispered, his hand poised above his weapon.

"Always," Morgan replied, her resolve steeling her nerves.

Together, they prepared to breach the threshold, to confront the darkness that waited on the other side. In that moment, they were not just partners, not just lovers—they were the last line of defense against a madness that sought to judge and execute with merciless precision.

***

Morgan's hand closed around the butt of her gun, a familiar weight settling in her palm as she waited for Derik to give the signal. With no answer at the door of Darren Reeves's house, they exchanged a look that needed no words. Both agents were primed for what might face them on the other side. It was time to break in.

Derik stepped back, driving his boot into the lock with practiced force. The door swung open with a violent creak, revealing the dimly lit hallway of Darren Reeves's home. They moved in, clearing corners with swift efficiency, their movements synchronized after countless hours of training together.

The air inside was stale, untouched by human presence for days, perhaps longer. A chill wrapped around Morgan's spine, not from the temperature, but from the sense of abandonment that clung to the place. Dust motes danced in the slanting light as they advanced, room by room. Each space they entered was methodically searched, but it was clear: He had already moved on.

"Looks like we're too late," Derik's voice was low, tinged with frustration.

"Let's keep looking. There might be something left behind," Morgan replied, her instincts refusing to let go. Her eyes scanned the environment for any sign, any clue that might have been overlooked.

In the last bedroom, the first thing that caught her eye was the wall. Newspaper clippings were haphazardly pinned and taped across the plaster, forming a macabre collage that chronicled their own case. Photos of the victims stared back at them, their final moments immortalized by press sensationalism. Headlines screamed details of the murders, each font larger and more lurid than the last.

"Jesus," Derik muttered beside her, his hands rubbing together in that nervous gesture that belied his calm exterior.

"Confirmation," Morgan said, her voice hollow. The killer's narrative was laid bare before them, a twisted roadmap of retribution. But the architect of this horror was absent, a ghost eluding capture. The realization that he was still out there, possibly enacting the next phase of his plan, sent a shiver down her spine.

"Let's get CSI in here. Maybe he left something else," she suggested, though the sinking feeling in her gut told her that Darren Reeves was far too meticulous to leave anything by accident.

As Derik called it in, Morgan lingered, studying the faces of the dead and the words that sealed their fates. This wasn't just a man grieving his sister; this was someone who had taken his pain and transformed it into a mission. A mission that they had to end before anyone else became a headline on a killer's wall.

***

Morgan's fingers flew across the keyboard in a staccato rhythm, her eyes scanning the plethora of tabs open on the computer screen. Files, records, reports—every shred of Darren Reeves's life sprawled before her as she sat hunched in the FBI headquarters' dimly lit room. The air was thick with urgency; Derik stood behind her, phone pressed to his ear, his voice a low murmur as he spoke with the hospital where Reeves worked.

"Nothing," he finally said, hanging up and meeting Morgan's gaze. "He hasn't shown up for three days."

"Three days," Morgan echoed, something cold and heavy settling in her stomach. She felt the weight of each second ticking by, aware that with every moment lost, Reeves could be plotting his next move. He had been right under their noses, wearing the mask of the bereaved brother so convincingly that she had almost let herself be swayed by his grief.

Almost.

She leaned back, rubbing at the tension knotting her neck and shoulders. Her dark brown hair fell around her face like a curtain, and she pushed it back irritably. Despite the chill of the room, sweat beaded at her temples—the product of adrenaline and a mind racing to connect the dots.

"He's been planning this for months," she murmured, more to herself than Derik. Her eyes were drawn again to the screen, to the bank statements showing withdrawals, the cash transactions too frequent to be coincidental. He had rented spaces, always in cash, never leaving a traceable footprint. Each victim had been chosen with chilling precision, their fates sealed by their past actions—or rather, their inactions.

Darren Reeves wasn't just inflicting pain; he was meting out his own twisted form of justice.

Morgan's thoughts drifted unbidden to her own past, to the years stolen from her, to the betrayal that had landed her in prison. She understood bitterness, the desire for vengeance. But where she had fought to clear her name, to bring down those who had wronged her, Reeves had built traps. He had constructed trials designed to force his victims to face the consequences of their apathy, the same way his sister had faced hers alone.

"Obsessed with justice," she finally broke the silence, her voice tinged with a bitterness born of experience. "Or his version of it."

Derik nodded, lines of strain etched into his face. They both knew what was at stake. They both understood that each revelation brought them closer to the man who had turned grief into a weapon, but also deeper into a maze with no clear exit.

"Let's get a list of all the short-term rentals paid in cash within the last year," Morgan said, standing up and stretching the stiffness from her limbs. Her movements were methodical, purposeful, mirroring the resolve tightening within her chest. She wouldn't let another tragedy unfold—not on her watch.

As they began to coordinate with local law enforcement, Morgan's mind was ablaze with the grim tableau of Reeves's vengeance. The trap rooms, the meticulously planned scenarios—it was all coming together in a narrative she wished she couldn't comprehend.

Morgan's thoughts turned to the countless preventable deaths Reeves had witnessed as a trauma nurse. His sister's suicide, a pivotal point of pain that seemed to have set him on this path of righteous fury. Each victim selected as a symbol, a stand-in for those who had bypassed the chance to intervene, to save a life. How many more had looked away? How many more scenes had etched themselves into Reeves' memory, fueling his compulsion to force others to face judgment?

She knew they were missing something crucial, a piece of the puzzle that remained obscured by the chaos of the investigation and their own desperate need to stop the killings. There was no telling how many traps were left or who might be the next to fall into his fatal embrace.

As she reached for another pin to add to the board, a phone rang, slicing through the tension. Derik, stationed at a nearby desk, answered it with his usual clipped efficiency. Morgan watched as his posture stiffened, the hand not holding the receiver clenching reflexively into a fist.

"Cross," he called out, voice sharpening with urgency. "A man survived one of Reeves' traps."

She straightened instantly, stepping toward him. "Who?" she demanded, her heart pounding a fierce rhythm against her ribs.

"Thomas Bryant," Derik replied, eyes locking with hers. "He's alive but barely conscious. They're rushing him to the ER now."

Morgan felt a surge of adrenaline. A survivor meant a witness, a chance to glean insight from someone who had experienced Reeves' twisted version of justice firsthand. But it also meant Reeves would be compelled to close that loose end to ensure no one escaped his verdict. They needed to act fast to protect Bryant and leverage any information he could provide.

"Let's move," she said, already heading for the door, Derik at her heels.

CHAPTER NINETEEN

Morgan entered the sterile chaos of the emergency room just as they wheeled him in. The gurney rushed past, a blur of motion and medical urgency, carrying Dr. Thomas Bryant—his body a roadmap of pain and narrowly-escaped death. The harsh lights illuminated his ashen face, each crease and shadow accentuating the proximity of his brush with mortality. His wrists were a mess of lacerations, hands sliced by shards of betrayal, while his skin held the pallor of a man who had danced a duet with the dark. Glass had been his unwilling partner, carbon monoxide the orchestra playing a silent symphony in his lungs, stealing his breath with merciless efficiency until fate or chance had intervened.

The metallic scent of blood mingled with antiseptic, a sensory reminder of the fragility of life that permeated the air around them.

"Cross," Derik murmured, close enough to share her space but far enough to watch the whirlwind of doctors and nurses descend upon the survivor. His voice carried the weight of their shared history, a shorthand developed through years of partnership and unspoken trust. Their eyes met, a silent conversation passing between them—Reeves had failed this time, but it was a temporary reprieve. The harshness of the hospital lighting carved deep shadows beneath Derik's cheekbones, accentuating the concern etched across his features. It was unlikely the trauma nurse turned executioner would allow his narrative to be disrupted by a living testament to his fallibility. Reeves's pride would demand completion, his warped sense of justice requiring the final period at the end of Bryant's sentence.

"Stay with Bryant," Morgan ordered, her tone brooking no argument, though her eyes softened for a moment as they lingered on Derik. The subtle shift in her expression spoke volumes—a vulnerability she allowed only him to glimpse, a momentary crack in her otherwise impenetrable armor. She trusted him to guard the doctor's fragile lifeline against an enemy who considered finality a virtue, who saw death not as the end but as the ultimate judgment. Turning away, she strode from the room, her mind already cataloging the next steps, calculating probabilities and mapping out the spider's web of Reeves's possible moves with the precision that had made her legendary within the Bureau before her fall from grace.

Her footsteps echoed through the corridor, keeping time with the urgent cadence of her thoughts. Each click of her boots against the linoleum floor was a metronome, setting the pace for this deadly game of cat and mouse they found themselves entangled in.

Outside the hospital, the afternoon sun bore down mercilessly, indifferent to the life-and-death drama unfolding within the manmade caverns of healing. The heat shimmered off the asphalt, creating ripples in the air like distortions in reality—not unlike the twisted mirror through which Reeves viewed his own actions. Morgan dialed the number of the local law enforcement liaison, her voice steady as she laid out their predicament, each word measured and deliberate, wasting nothing. "We need eyes on every property rented in cash over the last few months. Short-term leases, storage units, anywhere Reeves could have set up his judgment chambers."

"Understood, Agent Cross," came the crisp reply, laced with the respect her reputation commanded despite—or perhaps because of—her troubled history. Orders were dispatched, and a citywide search commenced. Each possible location held the potential for salvation or disaster—a race against an unseen countdown where the prize was human lives, the forfeit paid in blood and shattered futures.

As the net cast wider, Morgan felt a familiar coil of tension winding tighter within her, a serpent of anxiety and determination intertwined. She scanned the parking lot, cataloging faces, vehicles, movements—anything out of place, any shadow that might conceal a predator. The heat pressed against her skin, but she barely registered it, her focus razor-sharp and unwavering. Reeves was out there, planning his next move, perhaps already implementing it while they scrambled to catch up.

"Find him," she whispered to herself as she paced outside the ER, the words a promise and a prayer. Her eyes scanned the horizon for any sign of movement, any hint of the killer who thought himself an arbiter of fate. The afternoon light cast long shadows across the pavement, stretching like fingers reaching for the sanctuary of the hospital where Bryant fought for his life. Darren Reeves had made a fatal mistake underestimating Morgan Cross, and she intended to return the favor with interest, to show him the difference between his manufactured justice and the real thing.

***

The scent of rust and decay wafted through the air, a tangible miasma of abandonment and industrial decline that coated the back of Morgan's throat with each breath. She stood before the derelict building in the industrial district, a hulking skeleton of concrete and corroded metal that seemed to absorb the waning daylight rather than reflect it. The wind whistled through broken windows, creating an eerie melody that spoke of emptiness and desolation—the perfect stage for Reeves's macabre performances.

It was after hours of searching that local law enforcement finally got a hit, and she was here with Derik at her side, staring up at the structure that matched Reeves's pattern to the last twisted detail. The building itself seemed to hold secrets, its boarded windows like closed eyelids concealing horrors within. Graffiti marred the lower walls, urban hieroglyphics telling stories of territory and rebellion, now faded and chipped like ancient cave paintings.

"Team's ready on your go," Derik murmured, his voice low but steady, a constant in the chaos that had become their lives. His eyes scanned the boarded-up windows, his hand resting near his holstered weapon, fingers twitching with readiness born of years in the field. The late afternoon sun caught in his auburn hair, setting it ablaze with copper highlights that contrasted sharply with the grimness of their surroundings. The anticipation hung heavy around them, the stillness of the afternoon punctuated by the distant hum of city life, a reminder of the normality that continued unaware of the deadly game unfolding in its shadows.

Morgan felt the weight of decision pressing down on her shoulders, the lives that hung in the balance with every choice she made. The tactical team waited at a discreet distance, their black uniforms absorbing the light, their faces set in masks of professional determination. They trusted her judgment, followed her lead without question—a responsibility she carried like atlas with the world upon his back.

"Wait." Morgan's voice cut through the tension like a blade, sharp and decisive. She stepped closer to the map spread across the hood of their vehicle, her keen eyes tracing the streets, the dots marking potential trap rooms, their paths converging on this spot with a symmetry that now struck her as too perfect, too convenient. "Something isn't right."

Derik leaned in, his brow furrowing, creating deep lines across his forehead that spoke of countless similar moments of concentration. The scent of his aftershave mingled with the metallic tang of the air, familiar and grounding. "What is it?"

"Reeves..." She shook her head, frustration mounting as she tapped a finger against the map, against the X that marked their current location. Her instincts screamed warnings she couldn't ignore, alarms ringing in the recesses of her mind where intuition and experience intertwined. "This could just be a distraction."

The realization hit her with physical force, a punch to the gut that left her momentarily breathless. The pieces fell into place with terrifying precision—Reeves had led them here deliberately, away from his true target, like a magician directing attention to one hand while the other performed the trick.

"Are you sure?" Derik asked, but the question was mere formality. His body was already tensing, preparing for the shift in plans that would inevitably follow. He knew better than to doubt her. They had been through hell and back, their partnership a dance of trust and truth, each step choreographed by years of shared danger and mutual respect.

"Positive." Morgan's decision crystallized with sharp clarity, her mind racing ahead, anticipating Reeves's endgame with the clarity of someone who had stared into the abyss of human depravity and returned to tell the tale. "You take the team inside. I'm going back to the hospital. Bryant's not safe; Reeves will finish what he started."

The wind picked up, carrying with it the distant sound of sirens, an urban soundtrack to their unfolding drama. Loose debris skittered across the cracked concrete at their feet, dust devils dancing in miniature tornados before dissipating into nothing—ephemeral as the opportunity they now had to catch Reeves before he claimed another victim.

Derik met her gaze, concern etched across his features, lines deepening at the corners of his eyes. The bond between them, forged in the crucible of shared dangers and mutual protection, hummed with unspoken communication. "I don't like splitting up."

His words carried more than professional caution; they held the weight of personal fear, of knowing all too well the price of separation in their line of work.

"Neither do I." Her reply was firm, laced with urgency that brooked no argument, yet tender enough to acknowledge his concern. She placed a hand briefly on his arm, the contact brief but meaningful, a tangible connection to anchor them both. "But we have to cover both bases. He's playing us, Derik. We can't let him win."

With a curt nod, Derik relayed the change of plans to the team, his voice steady though she saw the worry flickering in his green eyes, a storm of emotion carefully contained behind professional composure. They were in uncharted waters, and the current was pulling them under fast, threatening to drown them in the consequences of missteps and miscalculations.

Morgan turned on her heel, every cell in her body urging her back to the hospital, every instinct screaming that time was running out. The gravel crunched beneath her boots as she strode toward the unmarked car, each step purposeful and charged with determination. She couldn't shake the image of Dr. Bryant's pale face, the barely-there breaths that fogged the oxygen mask in erratic patterns, each one a tenuous hold on life. Reeves had left a survivor, and if there was one thing she knew about men like him—they never left loose ends. They viewed unfinished business as personal affront, incomplete narratives as challenges to their authority as authors of others' fates.

She hailed an unmarked car, giving the driver clipped instructions that conveyed both urgency and authority. The agent behind the wheel nodded, recognizing the gravity in her tone, the life-or-death stakes that hung in the balance. As the vehicle sliced through the city, sirens concealed beneath its hood, Morgan replayed every interaction with Reeves, every word he had uttered, searching for clues she might have missed, patterns that could reveal his next move.

He'd appeared grief-stricken, shattered by the loss of his sister, his performance so convincing that even she—with all her hard-earned cynicism—had initially believed his pain genuine. But now she saw the cracks in his facade, the careful staging of a man hell-bent on delivering his version of justice, a perversion of the healing oath he had once taken as a medical professional. His grief was real, perhaps, but it had twisted into something monstrous, a justification for atrocities committed in the name of retribution.

Through the car window, the city blurred past—office buildings and apartments, restaurants and shops, lives continuing in blissful ignorance of the predator in their midst. The sunlight bounced off glass and metal, creating prisms and reflections that fragmented reality into kaleidoscopic patterns. Morgan's mind swirled with thoughts of her own quest for vengeance against those who had wronged her—against

Cordell and the corruption that had seeped into the very foundations of the Bureau, rotting it from within like a cancer.

But this—this was different. Darren Reeves was out there, claiming the role of judge and executioner, perverting the principles of justice she had devoted her life to upholding. His actions were not retribution but murder, not balance but bloodshed, and she wouldn't allow another tragedy on her watch. Not when she had the power to stop it, to intercept his hand before it dealt another fatal card.

The hospital loomed ahead, a towering beacon of light amidst the gathering dusk. Its countless windows glowed with artificial daylight, each one representing a life in transition—healing or ending, beginning or continuing. Somewhere within that labyrinth of corridors and rooms, Reeves was making his move, threading his way toward his prey with the precision of a surgeon and the intent of an assassin.

Morgan braced herself, shoulders squaring with resolve, jaw set with determination. She knew that within those walls, a killer sought to play god over life and death, to render verdict without trial, sentence without appeal. And she would be damned if she let him succeed, if she allowed him to claim another victim while she drew breath.

"Step on it," she urged the driver, her voice tight with controlled urgency, her body coiled with readiness for the confrontation to come. The early evening shadows lengthened across the dashboard as the car accelerated, eating up the distance between them and their destination. Her resolve steeled within her, a core of unbreakable purpose forged in the fires of her own suffering and tempered by the oath she had taken to protect others from the same. "We're running out of time."

***

Morgan's legs pumped like pistons as she hurtled down the hospital corridor. Her boots thudded against the linoleum, a staccato rhythm that punctuated her urgency, each impact sending jolts up her calves and into her thighs, pain she barely registered in her single-minded focus. Nurses and doctors turned, startled by the blur of an FBI agent barreling past them, her face set in a mask of determination that discouraged questions or interference. The fluorescent lights overhead flickered in her peripheral vision, casting a sterile glow on walls lined with sanitized hope, the antiseptic brightness exposing every detail with clinical precision—the worn edges of bulletin boards, the slight yellowing of once-white ceiling tiles, the smudged fingerprints on glass door panels.

The hospital sounds enveloped her—the soft ping of monitors, the hushed conversations of medical staff, the occasional announcement over the PA system—all processing in the background of her consciousness as irrelevant data. Her focus narrowed to a laser point: room 312, where Bryant lay vulnerable, where Reeves might already be completing his unfinished symphony of destruction. The air tasted of disinfectant and fear, her own adrenaline adding a metallic tang that coated her tongue with each ragged breath.

She rounded the corner so sharply that her shoulder brushed the wall, sending a jolt through her collarbone, the momentary pain registering as nothing more than a fleeting signal easily dismissed. Every second mattered; every heartbeat was a ticking clock in this race against a killer's twisted sense of justice. The corridor stretched before her, seemingly endless in her urgency, each door a potential barrier between her and her goal.

Her hand instinctively checked her weapon, the solid presence of the gun a reassurance against her hip. The weight of it grounded her, connected her to her purpose, to the oath she had taken to protect and serve, to be the shield between innocents and those who would prey upon them. In her mind, she saw Bryant's pale face, the life hanging by threads as fragile as spider silk, waiting for Reeves's scissors to make the final cut.

The number on Dr. Bryant's door loomed closer—312 in stark black against sterile white, each digit growing larger as she closed the distance with relentless momentum. Adrenaline flooded her system, sharpening her senses, preparing her for what lay beyond. The world narrowed to that single point in space and time, all else falling away as irrelevant, as background noise to the critical moment approaching with each stride. She reached for the handle, her breaths coming hard and fast, each one tasting of the cold resolve.

The metal of the door handle was cool against her palm, the sensation registering distantly as her muscles tensed in preparation. Time seemed to slow, each millisecond stretching into eternity as her fingers closed around the handle, as the latch gave way beneath her pressure. Her heart thundered in her chest, a war drum setting the pace for the battle to come.

She burst through the door.

CHAPTER TWENTY

Time seemed to elongate, stretching into a taut wire of horror. The moment froze in Morgan's perception, each detail etching itself into her memory with crystalline clarity. Darren Reeves stood over Dr. Bryant's bed, his tall frame hunched in predatory focus, his hands white-knuckled around a pillow pressed cruelly against the man's face. The murderous intent was palpable in the rigid line of his shoulders, in the trembling intensity of his grip. Dr. Bryant was a tableau of desperation beneath him, limbs flailing with the feeble strength of the nearly defeated, his body arching against the hospital bed in a desperate bid for oxygen. The IV tubes connected to his arms swung wildly with each movement, the life-giving fluids creating a macabre pendulum that marked the seconds of his fading existence. His fight was a silent scream that echoed in the sterile room, a muted plea that ricocheted off the clinical walls and pierced Morgan to her core.

The monitor beside the bed blared its frantic alarm, a shrill declaration of the life ebbing away beneath Reeves's merciless hands. The sound mingled with the ringing in Morgan's ears, creating a discordant symphony of imminent tragedy. The scent of antiseptic and clean linen was now tainted with the acrid stench of sweat and desperation—the unmistakable odor of a predator closing in for the kill.

"Reeves!" Morgan barked, her voice cutting through the muffled struggle like a knife, slicing through the tension with commanding authority that reverberated off the walls. The sound of her own voice seemed distant to her ears, as if coming from somewhere outside herself. She didn't hesitate, didn't falter. Her hand flew to her holster with instinctive precision born of years of training and life-or-death situations. Drawing her weapon with practiced ease, the familiar weight settling into her palm with the comfort of certainty. The gun was an extension of her will, a conduit for the justice she was sworn to uphold, the cold metal warming instantly to her touch as if recognizing its purpose in her hands.

His medical scrubs—the uniform of healing—now seemed a mockery, a disguise that had allowed the wolf to walk freely among the sheep.

"Step away from him, now!" Her aim was steady, unwavering as she leveled the barrel at Reeves. Her finger rested with practiced restraint against the trigger guard, ready to move with microsecond precision should the need arise. In her mind's eye, she saw not just the man before her but also the faces of those he had judged, those he had tormented with his delusions of righteousness—faces drawn in pain, contorted in final moments of terror and realization. And behind them all, the shadowy specter of Richard Cordell, the puppeteer of her past pains, the architect of her downfall, his influence a phantom that haunted every case she touched since her exoneration.

The room seemed to contract around the three of them—Morgan, Reeves, and Bryant—the outside world fading into irrelevance. The steady drip of the IV, the distant sounds of hospital activity beyond the door, all receded into background noise, insignificant against the life-or-death drama unfolding in this sterile chamber.

"Let him go," she commanded, each word a hammer strike against the silence, reverberating with the force of her conviction and the steel of her resolve. Her voice did not waver, did not betray the thundering of her heart or the surge of adrenaline coursing through her veins.

Reeves's gaze met hers, two sets of eyes locked in a battle of wills across the sterile battlefield of the hospital room. In his eyes, she saw the reflection of her own darkness—the consuming need for retribution, the bitter taste of betrayal, the corrosive power of grief that ate away at one's soul until nothing remained but hollow purpose. But where he had surrendered to the darkness, she had found her way back, clawing her way through ten years of wrongful imprisonment to reclaim her humanity, her purpose.

Morgan's resolve was ironclad. She would not blink. She would not yield. Not to him, not to the echoes of Cordell that still haunted her dreams, not to the shadows of doubt that sometimes whispered in her darkest moments.

Morgan's heart hammered against her ribcage, each beat a war drum that reverberated through her body. The gun in her hand was an anchor in a sea of chaos, its weight a reminder of her duty, her purpose, her oath to protect. Reeves stood motionless before her, his ragged breaths filling the room with the sound of shattered restraint. They came in harsh gasps, each one carrying the weight of his fractured psyche, the culmination of a journey that had led him from healer to destroyer. He clutched the pillow tightly, his knuckles white with strain, a monument to his crumbling conviction. The fabric was indented with the impression of his fingers, creased by the force of his grip, a physical manifestation of how tightly he clung to his distorted sense of justice.

"Drop it, Reeves," she ordered again, her voice lowered to a steady, dangerous timbre that brooked no argument. But her words were swallowed by the tension that gripped the room like a vice, seeming to dissipate into the sterile air without reaching their target. The machine monitoring Bryant's vitals continued its urgent beeping, the rhythm now erratic, a digital countdown to potential tragedy.

For a heartbeat, or perhaps an eternity, nothing moved.

The scene was frozen in terrible potential—a tableau of life suspended at the precipice of death. He could still do it—end Bryant's life and complete the deranged cycle he had set into motion, fulfill what he saw as his sacred duty of judgment and retribution.

Morgan saw the calculation in his eyes, the desperate mathematics of a man weighing his own twisted principles against the barrel of her gun. A man who had seen too much death was now the harbinger of it, lost in his own twisted sense of justice, drowning in the belief that his pain gave him the right to inflict suffering on others.

The muscles in his face twitched with indecision, with the internal war raging behind his eyes. Sweat beaded on his forehead, catching the harsh light from above, turning each droplet into a miniature prism. His chest heaved with labored breath, each inhalation shuddering through his frame as if his body was rebelling against the mind that drove it to such extremes.

Then, as if the strings holding him together had been cut by some invisible hand, the tension in Reeves's shoulders unraveled. The rigid posture collapsed inward, deflating like a balloon pricked by the needle of reality. His grip slackened, fingers uncurling one by one from their death hold, and the pillow fell from his hands like a discarded confession, fluttering to the floor with a soft thud that seemed to echo in the charged silence. The furious determination that once fueled him seemed to evaporate, leaving behind only the hollow shell of a broken man, a vessel emptied of purpose and filled only with the ashes of misguided vengeance.

A shuddering breath escaped Bryant as the pressure lifted, his chest rising in desperate hunger for air. The immediate crisis passed, but the shadow of what had almost happened lingered like a phantom in the room, a specter of averted tragedy.

Morgan kept her weapon trained on him, her stance unwavering despite the relief that flooded her system. She maintained her focus with the discipline that had carried her through countless confrontations, even as officers flooded the room, a swarm of blue and black that engulfed Reeves in swift efficiency. Their footsteps thundered against the linoleum, voices calling out commands that overlapped in controlled chaos. The air filled with the rustle of tactical gear, the click of handcuffs, the authoritative voices of law enforcement taking control of the situation.

They didn't need to use force; he offered no resistance as they cuffed his hands behind his back, the metal bracelets closing around his wrists with a definitive click that seemed to punctuate the end of his reign of terror. Eyes shut, Reeves exhaled, a long, deliberate breath that seemed to drain all remaining fight from his body, leaving him diminished and defeated. It was a surrender without words, a capitulation to the fate he had once sought to control, an acknowledgment that his self-appointed role as judge and executioner had come to its inevitable conclusion.

The officers flanking him cast questioning glances at Morgan, silently deferring to her authority despite her complicated history with the Bureau. It was a small validation, a recognition of her redemption that might have pleased her under different circumstances.

Watching him, Morgan felt no triumph, no surge of satisfaction at having captured the killer who had terrorized the city. There was no victory in witnessing a man succumb to the very despair he had inflicted upon others, no joy in seeing another life derailed by grief and vengeance.

The adrenaline began to ebb from her system, leaving behind a bone-deep weariness that settled into every fiber of her being. Yet beneath the fatigue, a spark of relief flickered—Bryant would live, Reeves would face justice, and the cycle, for now, was broken.

Medical staff rushed past her to attend to Bryant, their movements swift and practiced as they checked vital signs, adjusted equipment, and murmured reassurances to their barely conscious colleague. The room transformed into a hub of activity, of healing rather than harm, reclaiming its purpose from the darkness that had momentarily claimed it.

Reeves was led away, his footsteps muted against the linoleum, each step seeming to require tremendous effort, as if he carried the weight of his victims on his shoulders. His head was bowed, not in shame but in exhaustion, in the final surrender of a battle fought too long and at too great a cost. Morgan remained standing, the echo of her father's words from the shack in the woods mingling with the ghostly whispers of Cordell's machinations. This was not the end, not for her. The shadows cast by her past were long, and though one threat lay neutralized, others lurked just out of sight, patient predators waiting for their moment to strike.

She took a deep breath, steadying herself against the unending tide of darkness that seemed to lap at the shores of her life, threatening to pull her under with each case, each confrontation, each reminder of the corruption that had stolen a decade of her existence. Richard Cordell was still out there, a specter of retribution, and Morgan Cross knew her war was far from over, the final reckoning still to come, the ultimate accounting for past sins still pending. But for now, the immediate danger had passed, and another twisted soul had been stopped from meting out his perverse brand of justice, from playing god with lives that were not his to take.

The cold lights cast her shadow long against the hospital floor, stretching it into something almost unrecognizable—a reminder of how easily shapes could distort, how quickly justice could become vengeance, how thin the line between protector and predator truly was.

Morgan watched as Darren Reeves, now a shadow of the man who once stood confidently in his scrubs, shuffled between two stone-faced officers. His shoulders were slumped in defeat, his once-purposeful stride reduced to the halting gait of the condemned. The stark contrast between who he had been—a respected trauma nurse, a healer by profession and calling—and what he had become was jarring, a disturbing reminder of how far the human spirit could fall when pushed beyond its breaking point.

Shadows danced across his features, accentuating the hollows beneath his cheekbones, the dark circles under his eyes—physical manifestations of the spiritual void that had consumed him.

His voice, when he spoke, cracked the sterile silence with a raw edge that clawed at Morgan's insides, a sound so filled with pain that it seemed to physically manifest in the air between them. It was a voice scraped raw by grief, by the corrosive power of loss left to fester without resolution.

"It was Sarah," he began, each word laced with the poison of loss, dripping with the venom of abandonment that had corrupted his soul. The name fell from his lips like a sacred invocation, a talisman against the darkness that had claimed him. "Sarah's suicide... it broke me." His voice caught on the word 'suicide,' as if the mere utterance of it tore open wounds that had never truly healed, exposing the festering grief beneath the veneer of control.

Morgan's gaze didn't waver, her dark brown eyes fixed on him, absorbing every confession like a sentence to her own soul. She recognized the pain that radiated from him, understood the devastating power of loss to reshape a person, to carve them into something unrecognizable even to themselves. Her own losses—her freedom, her reputation, years of her life stolen by corruption—had nearly broken her, had tempted her down similar paths of revenge and retribution. The parallels were not lost on her, the mirror image of what she might have become had circumstances been slightly different, had her moral compass shifted just a few degrees further into the darkness.

Reeves' face twisted in pain as he recounted years spent at the edge of life and death, his hands often the last line of defense against the inevitable. The muscles around his eyes contracted, creating a web of lines that aged him beyond his years. His lips trembled with the effort of containing emotions too vast, too overwhelming to be fully expressed in mere words. The story spilled from him now, a dam broken after years of silent pressure building behind it.

"I tried to save them—people who shouldn't have died," he continued, his voice gaining strength from the embers of his smoldering grief, each word propelled by the righteous indignation that had fueled his crusade. His hands, now restrained behind his back, twitched as if remembering the countless times they had worked to staunch bleeding, restart hearts, bring life back from the brink—and later, to deliver his twisted version of justice. "But Sarah..." He choked on the name, the image of his sister too much to bear, the wound of her loss still gaping and raw despite the years that had passed. The name hung in the air between them, a ghost that refused to be laid to rest.

"Nobody saved her," he whispered, the words barely audible yet somehow filling the corridor with their weight. "Hawthorne saw her note, knew she was in agony... and he did nothing. Just walked away." The last three words were spoken with such venom, such burning hatred that they seemed to physically heat the air between them. His eyes, when they met Morgan's again, burned with the intensity of his conviction, with the belief that had driven him to become the very monster he had sought to punish.

Morgan's heart clenched at his words, a physical reaction to the pain that radiated from him in palpable waves. Despite everything he had done, despite the lives he had taken in his quest for twisted justice, she couldn't help but feel a flicker of understanding—not sympathy, not acceptance, but a recognition of the human tragedy that lay at the core of his transformation. She thought of her father, hidden away in the woods, a man who had retreated from the world rather than engage with its corruption. She thought of Thomas and the cruel twist of fate that had made them siblings only in death, united by blood they never knew they shared until it was too late. The tangled webs of vengeance and justice seemed to constrict around her, suffocating in their complexity, in the way they intertwined and overlapped until distinguishing between them became an impossible task.

The corridor seemed to narrow around them, the walls closing in as if the weight of his confession physically altered the space they occupied. The distant sounds of the hospital—phones ringing, elevators chiming, the low murmur of conversations—created a surreal backdrop to the intensely personal revelation unfolding in this sterile hallway.

"Michelle Knox," Reeves spat out the name like venom, each syllable dripping with contempt, with the loathing that had festered in his soul until it poisoned every aspect of his being. His eyes glazed with the memory, looking beyond Morgan to a past only he could see, recounting the story of the woman who had passed by a dying man without a second glance, her apathy a criminal offense in his twisted code of morality. "They all turned their backs. I had to make them understand what it feels like... to be judged."

The last word hung in the air, a declaration of his self-appointed role, of the power he had assumed over life and death. It was said without apology, without remorse—a final assertion of the righteousness that had guided his hand through each meticulously planned judgment, each execution disguised as poetic justice.

The room seemed to contract around Morgan, the air heavy with the weight of consequences, with the accumulated pain of lives destroyed by grief compounding upon grief, vengeance breeding vengeance in an endless cycle.

As Reeves was led away, Morgan felt the sharp sting of revelation piercing through the haze of the investigation, cutting to the heart of what this case truly represented. This wasn't a victory; this was a cycle of tragedy perpetuating itself—a vicious circle where grief bred vengeance and justice was lost in the fray, where victims became victimizers and the line between right and wrong blurred beyond recognition.

The officers guided Reeves around a corner, his confession still echoing in the empty corridor, his presence lingering like a specter even after he had physically departed. Morgan remained motionless, the weight of what had transpired settling over her like a heavy cloak. Her muscles ached with tension finally released, with the aftermath of adrenaline that left her drained yet hyperaware, exhausted yet unable to rest.

The case might be closed, the killer apprehended, but the resolution brought no peace, no sense of completion or closure. It was just another entry in the ledger of human suffering, another story where the lines between hero and villain blurred beyond recognition, where tragedy spawned tragedy in an endless ripple effect that touched countless lives. The knowledge sat heavy in her chest, a weight that pressed against her lungs with each breath.

She knew there would always be another Darren Reeves, someone else pushed past the brink, convinced of their right to adjudicate the sins of others. Another soul twisted by circumstance and pain until they emerged on the other side as something monstrous, something barely recognizable as human. Another killer wrapped in the guise of judge and executioner, wielding pain as a weapon, using suffering as a currency to balance accounts that could never truly be settled. And the thought chilled her more than the cold grip of the gun she had pointed at a broken man moments ago, more than the antiseptic air of the hospital that now seemed to freeze in her lungs.

The hallway stretched before her, endless in its sterile emptiness, a metaphor for the path she still had to walk, for the journey that had no true destination, only milestones of varying pain and triumph. Her reflection caught in a darkened window—a solitary figure standing at the crossroads of justice and vengeance, duty and desire, past and future. The woman who stared back at her was both familiar and strange, both the person she had been before prison and someone entirely new, forged in the crucible of suffering and emerged stronger, if not unscathed.

As she left the room, her footsteps echoing in the empty corridor like a metronome counting out the rhythm of her thoughts, her mind turned inexorably to Cordell, to the unfinished business lurking in the shadows of her past.

She pushed open the door to the stairwell, preferring its utilitarian solitude to the forced sociality of the elevator. The concrete steps echoed with her descent, each footfall a punctuation mark in the ongoing narrative of her life. The metal handrail was cool beneath her palm, grounding her in the physical world when her thoughts threatened to spiral into the abstract realm of justice and morality.

Even then, as the hollow victory settled in her bones, seeping into the marrow with the cold certainty of truth, she knew the reality that faced her, faced all who stood on the thin line between order and chaos. The next time, they might not be so fortunate. The next killer might not hesitate, might not surrender to the humanity that still lurked somewhere within Reeves's broken soul. The next victim might not survive long enough for rescue, might become just another statistic, another name in the endless ledger of lives cut short by violence and malice.

And the realization gnawed at her, an ever-present specter whispering of darker days to come, of battles yet unfought, of monsters still lurking in the shadows of humanity's collective soul. It was a weight she carried with each step down the sterile stairwell, a burden she had shouldered the moment she reclaimed her badge, her purpose, her place in the unending war against the darkness that threatened to consume the world one broken soul at a time.

EPILOGUE*

Morgan sat alone, her eyes fixed on the whiteboard before her. Crime scene photos stared back, a grim collage of death and judgment. In the center, Darren Reeves's mugshot glared out at her, his eyes burning with righteous fury even in stillness.

Morgan's fingers traced the edge of her desk, the cool metal grounding her as Reeves's words echoed in her mind. "They had to face their failures," he had said, his voice dripping with contempt. "Someone had to hold them accountable."

She shook her head, trying to dislodge the memory, but it clung to her like a shadow. "Dammit," she muttered, pushing back from the desk with a screech of chair legs on linoleum. She paced the length of the room, her boots echoing in the silence.

How many times had she stood in this very room, feeling the weight of a case slipping through her fingers? How many times had she watched justice—real justice—dance just out of reach?

She stopped in front of the whiteboard, her eyes locking with Reeves's photograph. "You thought you were doing the right thing, didn't you?" she whispered, her voice barely audible over the hum of the lights. "You thought you were serving justice when the system failed."

Morgan's reflection ghosted over the glossy surface of the photos, her features superimposing over Reeves's for a heartbeat. The similarity made her stomach churn.

"But I'm not like you," she said, her voice growing stronger. "I won't cross that line. I can't."

Yet even as the words left her lips, doubt gnawed at her. How thin was that line, really? How many times had she been tempted to take matters into her own hands, especially after her wrongful imprisonment?

She thought of Richard Cordell, of the corruption that had stolen a decade of her life. Of Thomas, gunned down on that pier. Of her father, hidden away in the woods, a ghost from a past she thought long buried.

Morgan's fist clenched at her side. "The system failed me, too," she murmured, her eyes never leaving Reeves's photograph. "But I'm still here, still fighting. That's the difference between us, Reeves. I haven't given up on justice, not yet."

She turned away from the board, her gaze sweeping over the empty room. The weight of unsolved cases, of unpunished crimes, seemed to press down on her shoulders. But mixed with that familiar burden was something else—a spark of determination, a fire that had been rekindled by this case.

The soft squeak of chair wheels broke Morgan's reverie. She glanced up to see Derik settling into the seat across from her, his green eyes shadowed with concern. His normally slicked-back hair was slightly disheveled, a testament to the long hours they'd both put in on the Reeves case.

Derik leaned back, arms crossed over his chest, watching her with the quiet intensity that had become so familiar over their years as partners. Morgan felt a twinge of guilt; she knew he was worried about her, about the walls she'd been building between them lately.

The silence stretched, neither of them willing to break it first. Morgan's gaze drifted back to the whiteboard, to Reeves's mugshot staring back at her. She could feel Derik's eyes on her, patient, waiting.

Finally, he spoke, his voice low and gravelly with fatigue. "You need rest, Morgan. We both do."

She turned back to him, noting the lines of exhaustion etched around his eyes. "I know," she admitted, surprising herself with how easily the words came. "I just... I can't shake this feeling. Like we're missing something."

Derik leaned forward, elbows on his knees. "We got him, Morgan. Reeves is behind bars. It's over."

"Is it?" she murmured, more to herself than to him. She shook her head, trying to clear the fog of fatigue and doubt. "You're right. I need sleep. We both do."

A ghost of a smile touched Derik's lips. "There's the voice of reason I've been missing."

Morgan felt an answering smile tug at her own mouth, despite the heaviness in her chest. "Don't get used to it. I'm sure I'll be back to my stubborn self after a few hours of sleep."

Derik stood, stretching his tall frame. "I've got a few errands to run, but I'll stop by your place later. Make sure you're actually resting and not burning the midnight oil on some new lead."

"I promise," Morgan said, gathering her things. "I'll be there, probably passed out on the couch with Skunk using me as a pillow."

As she stood, the weight of the case seemed to settle on her shoulders like a physical thing. She could feel Derik watching her, could sense the questions he wasn't asking. How much should she tell him about her father, about Cordell? The secrets pressed against her tongue, begging to be shared.

Instead, she forced a smile. "I'll see you later, then?"

Derik nodded, his eyes never leaving hers. "Count on it."

Morgan headed for the door, feeling the pull of exhaustion with every step. As she reached the threshold, she paused, looking back at Derik. He was still watching her, concern etched in every line of his face.

"Derik," she said softly. "Thank you. For everything."

He nodded, a warmth in his eyes that made her heart ache. As she stepped out into the corridor, Morgan couldn't shake the feeling that something was shifting, that the ground beneath her feet was no longer as solid as she'd once believed. But for now, sleep called, and she had promises to keep.

***

The city lights blurred into a hazy glow as Morgan navigated the rain-slicked streets. Her grip on the steering wheel tightened, knuckles white against the black leather. The case might be closed, but the weight of it still pressed down on her, mingling with the exhaustion that seemed to seep into her very bones.

"Get it together, Cross," she muttered to herself, rolling her shoulders in a futile attempt to ease the tension.

As she pulled into her driveway, the porch light flickered to life, triggered by the motion sensor. Morgan sat for a moment, staring at the front door of her home. It should have felt welcoming, but something about it set her nerves on edge.

"You're just tired," she told herself, forcing her body into motion. "Derik's right. You need sleep."

She grabbed her bag and stepped out into the damp night air. The scent of rain lingered, heavy and oppressive. Morgan fumbled with her keys, the silence pressing in around her. It wasn't until she pushed open the front door that she realized what was wrong.

Silence. Complete and utter silence.

"Skunk?" she called out, her voice sounding unnaturally loud in the darkened house. "Here, boy."

Nothing. No click of nails on hardwood, no excited whine, no wagging tail thumping against the wall. Morgan's hand instinctively moved to her hip, fingers brushing against her holstered weapon.

"This isn't right," she thought, her mind racing through possibilities. "He always comes. Always."

Her FBI training kicked in, every sense on high alert. She moved carefully through the entryway, eyes scanning for any sign of disturbance. The house felt wrong, the air thick with an unseen threat.

"Skunk?" she called again, softer this time. Her free hand reached for the light switch, hesitating for just a moment before flicking it on.

The sudden brightness revealed nothing out of place, but it did nothing to ease the knot of dread forming in her stomach. Morgan's thoughts turned to Cordell, to her father's warnings. Had she been too careless? Too confident?

"Focus," she chided herself. "Clear the house. Find Skunk. Then worry about the rest."

But as she moved deeper into her home, Morgan couldn't shake the feeling that everything was about to change. Again. And this time, she wasn't sure she was ready for what was coming.

Then, a soft whine pierced the silence. Morgan's head snapped towards the sound, her heart pounding. A lamp flickered to life in the living room, casting long shadows across the floor. Every muscle in her body locked into place as she turned, her hand gripping her gun.

The sight that greeted her made her blood run cold.

Richard Cordell sat on her couch, legs crossed, exuding an air of calm expectation.

NOW AVAILABLE!

FOR VENGEANCE
(A Morgan Cross FBI Suspense Thriller—Book Seventeen)

FBI Agent Morgan Cross faces her most elusive adversary yet: a murderer who delivers final verdicts to criminals in the act. To stop the bloodshed, she'll have to think like a criminal and weave through moral quandaries that hit uncomfortably close to home—a deadly game of cat and mouse where every move could be her last.

"A masterpiece of thriller and mystery."
—Books and Movie Reviews, Roberto Mattos (re Once Gone)

FOR VENGEANCE is book #17 in a long-anticipated new series by #1 bestseller and USA Today bestselling author Blake Pierce, whose bestseller Once Gone (a free download) has received over 7,000 five star ratings and reviews.

Superstar FBI Agent Morgan Cross was at the height of her career when she was framed, wrongly imprisoned, and sent to do 10 hard years in prison. Finally exonerated and set free, Morgan emerges from jail as a changed person—hardened, ruthless, closed off to the world, and unsure how to start again. When the FBI comes knocking, desperately needing Morgan to return and hunt down a killer who seems to be obsessed with drowning, Morgan is torn.

Morgan is not the same person, no longer willing to play by the rules, and will stop at nothing this time. In a non-stop thriller, it will be a deadly cat and mouse chase between a diabolical killer and an ex-con FBI agent who has nothing left to lose—with a new victim's fate riding on it all.

A page-turning and harrowing crime thriller featuring a brilliant and tortured FBI agent, the Morgan Cross series is a riveting mystery, packed with non-stop action, suspense, twists and turns, revelations, and driven by a breakneck pace that will keep you flipping pages late into the night. Fans of Rachel Caine, Teresa Driscoll and Robert Dugoni are sure to fall in love.

Future books in the series are now available!

"An edge of your seat thriller in a new series that keeps you turning pages! ...So many twists, turns and red herrings… I can't wait to see what happens next."
—Reader review (Her Last Wish)

"A strong, complex story about two FBI agents trying to stop a serial killer. If you want an author to capture your attention and have you guessing, yet trying to put the pieces together, Pierce is your author!"
—Reader review (Her Last Wish)

"A typical Blake Pierce twisting, turning, roller coaster ride suspense thriller. Will have you turning the pages to the last sentence of the last chapter!!!"
—Reader review (City of Prey)

"Right from the start we have an unusual protagonist that I haven't seen done in this genre before. The action is nonstop… A very atmospheric novel that will keep you turning pages well into the wee hours."
—Reader review (City of Prey)

"Everything that I look for in a book… a great plot, interesting characters, and grabs your interest right away. The book moves along at a breakneck pace and stays that way until the end. Now on go I to book two!"
—Reader review (Girl, Alone)

"Exciting, heart pounding, edge of your seat book… a must read for mystery and suspense readers!"
—Reader review (Girl, Alone)

Blake Pierce

USA Today and #1 bestselling author Blake Pierce is the author of numerous series in the mystery and thriller genres, spanning 10 years of work, including the Jessie Hunt, Ella Dark, Rylie Page, Faith Bold and Rachel Gift series. Blake's most recent latest releases are the Jenna Graves, Alison Payne, Isla Rivers and Kari Blackhorse series.

Please visit blakepierceauthor.com to learn more, join the email list, receive free books, and stay in touch.

SERIES BY BLAKE PIERCE

KARI BLACKHORSE
ISLA RIVERS
ALISON PAYNE
JENNA GRAVES
THE GOVERNESS
RACHEL BLACKWOOD
SHEILA STONE
FINN WRIGHT
MORGAN CROSS
JULIETTE HART
FAITH BOLD
FIONA RED
DAISY FORTUNE
AMBER YOUNG
CAMI LARK
NICKY LYONS
CORA SHIELDS
MAY MOORE
PAIGE KING
VALERIE LAW
RACHEL GIFT
AVA GOLD
A YEAR IN EUROPE
ELLA DARK
LAURA FROST
EUROPEAN VOYAGE
ADELE SHARP
THE AU PAIR
ZOE PRIME
JESSIE HUNT
CHLOE FINE
KATE WISE
THE MAKING OF RILEY PAIGE
RILEY PAIGE
MACKENZIE WHITE
AVERY BLACK
KERI LOCKE

Printed in Great Britain
by Amazon

62778576R00082